THE URBANA FREE LIBRARY
3 1230 00469 8664

D0966666

Beth waited in the car while Helen strode around Aunt Ruth's house. She'd forgotten to get a key. Maybe it wasn't locked, she thought. But the front door rattled and withstood her attempts to open it. This was a big mistake, Helen thought as she walked around to the back door. She should come back alone tomorrow.

The back door resisted her efforts. With an angry sigh Helen crouched down to peer at the gray stone blocks that showed through the dirt, dismayed at the dilapidated condition of the house. It would take a long time to get it ready to sell, and even then —

Helen shuddered as a sudden chill swept over her body. She groped behind her until her hand found a loose stick. Carefully she poked and prodded at the clumps of earth that clung to the slender length of white fabric. As the soil fell away, the white fragment loosened and fell free. The shape, the length, the joint in the center — nausea gripped Helen as she realized what kind of remains she was looking at. She dropped the stick, backed away from the house and shouted for Beth.

Books in the
HELEN BLACK MYSTERY SERIES
by Pat Welch

MURDER BY THE BOOK
STILL WATERS
A PROPER BURIAL
OPEN HOUSE

Open House

A Helen Black Mystery by Pat Welch

THE NAIAD PRESS, INC.
1995

Printed in the United States of America on acid-free paper
First Edition

Edited by Christine Cassidy
Cover design by Bonnie Liss (Phoenix Graphics)
Typeset by Sandi Stancil

Library of Congress Cataloging-in-Publication Data

Welch, Pat, 1957 –
Open house : a Helen Black mystery / by Pat Welch.
p. cm.
ISBN 1-56280-102-3
I. Title.
PS3573.E4543064 1995
813′.54—dc20 94-43992
CIP

Dedicated to Paulette Washington
with gratitude and affection, and
with extra thanks to Brian Earle,
lesbianus emeritus

About the Author

Pat Welch was born in Japan in 1957. When her family returned to the United States, she lived in a series of small towns in the South. She relocated to northern California in 1986. *Open House* is the fourth novel in the Helen Black mystery series.

August 8, 1959

She didn't stop running until the water sloshed up over her ankles, the high-heeled shoes bought especially for the party forgotten in the mud about half a mile back. She felt, rather than saw, the rips and tears in the new dress — the dress Mama had spent so long on, making sure each and every seam was perfect, no strands hanging loose. Now the satiny white cloth laced with gold filaments hung off her, thin threads of shimmering color against the dank foliage around the river. The Big Black, smaller and quieter than its cousin a few miles away, lay still under a moonless sky, lapping at her feet as she struggled along the slippery bank. Once she slid, red mud smearing her legs and hips. Almost sinking into the water, she managed to grab hold of some sort of thick, strong weed and pull herself back toward the river's edge.

She shivered as she lay in the mud and listened for the sounds of running feet in the undergrowth, the slurry cries and catcalls that signaled a white man's drunken hilarity—bone-chilling sounds that presaged a lynching. As she lay there trying to catch her breath, a hoot owl intoned its mournful chant. That, the gurgle of sluggish water, and her own ragged gasps for air were the only noises she heard. For a moment the clouds that had warned of rain all afternoon parted, and the August moon, low and heavy and yellow, hung over her like a pale ghostly eye. She realized that the party dress would be highly visible in that light, so with her last reserves of energy she struggled back into the wet vines and weeds along the river until her own black skin melded into the darkness.

Minutes passed. Hope began to surge up as the silence continued. Waiting was hard. She kept remembering the events that had bought her to where she now was, cowering in the mud. If only she hadn't gone out of the house with Joe Nathan! It had been impossible to resist those velvet eyes, the slow smile, that way he had of just barely touching you and somehow promising so much with that touch. All the other girls in her tenth-grade class had stared after her with envy as she strolled past with the captain of the basketball team and the heart-throb of every girl in school.

"You mean you've never had a beer?" Joe Nathan had asked, his soft eyes widening in astonishment.

She'd laughed at his amazement. "Now, how's a good girl like me gonna get a beer? You know my mama will tan my hide for sure, she ever find out you been talking like this to me." But the words had come out soft, sweet, shy, clearly encouraging him to go on.

"Man, this is too much, too much." He shook his head in horror, making her laugh even more. "I mean, this is serious business now! Y'all can't be goin' to no more sweet-sixteen parties without a beer."

Without realizing quite how it happened, she followed him outside to where he said he'd parked his truck. As they got farther and farther away from the house, the music and laughter of her friends drifted off into the trees, and the bright squares of light coming from the windows seemed to glide in and out of the woods until they, too, disappeared. He stopped and took her hand.

"Where's the truck?" she asked, glancing around for its familiar shape. She didn't see the battered green hulk anywhere.

"We'll get there directly." His grip on her hand tightened, and something in his voice made her turn around and look at him. She couldn't see his face in the dark.

"What's the matter, Joe Nathan?" Her voice had come out all trembly, and she tried to pull her hand away.

It only made him pull her closer. "Nothin' wrong you can't fix for me, baby," he murmured. His hands were clasped behind her back now, and she breathed in the stink of cheap liquor — she'd been so dazzled by his attentions that she hadn't detected it before. "We don't need no beer," and his wet mouth found her neck.

She felt such an overwhelming revulsion she thought she might be sick. "No, Joe Nathan! Please!" What she'd meant to be a firm refusal emerged as a frightened whine. He laughed again. "They'll come looking for us, they gonna start wondering where we are —"

"Not for a while yet," he said, his hot breath grazing her ear. "Just take it easy, honey. I ain't gonna forget your beer."

Terrified, she started to scratch and claw. His grip began to hurt. It wasn't until his body froze against her that she heard what stopped his clumsy fumblings.

"Well, looky here what we got!"

White blazing light seemed to fill the sky, and she staggered as Joe Nathan released her. A sharp-edged rock gouged her knee as she stumbled, making her cry out as she struggled to stand. She couldn't tell how many there were standing in the circle. Several of them seemed to be holding flashlights. Or maybe there were a couple of cars pulled up, headlights glaring in at them. She remembered looking up at Joe Nathan and realizing with cold horror that he was just as frightened as she was and completely helpless to protect her, even if he'd wanted to. She remembered the clink of beer bottles in the awful silence.

"Looks like we got us a coupla coons ready to fuck, don't we?" Jeers and hoots followed this question.

She turned, trying to see, all the while feeling a strange unreality. As if in a dream, she heard the sniggering, the shuffling steps, the laughter.

"Hey, betcha he's got a boner in there. Wanna take a look?" More howls of laughter. "No, no, it's a scientific experiment," the voice said in mock severity. "Now listen, y'all, I just want to prove, once and for all — as a scientific fact — whether or not these niggers are as big as they say."

Joe Nathan started moaning in a high-pitched whine. She knew he was trembling uncontrollably.

"How 'bout it, boy?" A dark figure stopped in front of the light. She made out a dim shape looming larger and larger. Other shapes moved forward, weaving crazy patterns against the painful glare. "Can't you get it up now?"

Suddenly she fell to the ground, her cheek stinging and her eyes watering. She realized she'd been slapped.

"What about this one?" a different voice asked. "She looks kinda young."

"Oh, they start 'em out young," the first voice said. "We'll get to her in a minute."

A hand jerked her by the wrist and she lurched forward, bending her foot back so that her shoe loosened and slipped off. Without conscious thought she grabbed the shoe with her free hand and thrust its heel down into the hand that gripped her own.

"Goddamn bitch!" he howled.

She dropped back down to the ground and slithered away, moving so quickly she couldn't see anything.

"I'm gonna kill that nigger!" a voice bellowed behind her.

She had surprise on her side, though, as well as her attackers' advanced state of drunkenness. They made so much noise stumbling around that her own terrified crashing through the woods more than masked her escape. For a moment she thought of Joe Nathan and stopped in her tracks. But it was only a moment. The memory of his hot stinking breath filled her with fear again. "I've got to find somebody. I've got to get somebody," she whispered over and over again. "Sweet Jesus, help me find somebody."

She'd been practically knee-deep in the Big Black before she slowed down. If she kept going east, she knew, she'd reach Tom Johnson's house. He'd know what to do, she told herself as she lay there in the mud. He was a smart man, taught in the school, even preached once in a while — he'd think of some way to help get Joe Nathan away from those men.

The owl had either moved on or lapsed into silence. Everything was absolutely still. She lifted herself up a few inches, waited a few more minutes, then began to walk on violently shaking legs. Every few steps she'd stop and listen, only to have her straining ears take in the sound of the water sucking at the mud. The moon played tag with the clouds and a cool wind came up. Rain spattered in huge drops as the storm finally broke.

She lifted her swollen face to the sky. No thunder, no lightning — just a thick mist of warm spray.

"Hey," a deep voice said. He was just a few feet behind her. She was too shocked to cry out. Even if she had, it wouldn't have mattered. There was no one to hear, no one to see. The worst part was, she knew that voice.

The leaves and tall grasses behind her shifted, swayed in the rain. He was coming.

Chapter One

Helen glanced up at the clock on the wall behind her lover's head. "Quit worrying," Frieda said. "Your flight doesn't leave for another twenty minutes." She peered over her coffee mug at the drink in Helen's hand. "Any more of those and I'll have to pour you down the terminal."

Helen turned away to look at the people milling through the airport. "I always wonder where everyone is going. Or coming from."

"Well, I doubt they'll all be going to Mississippi

with you." Helen caught Frieda's smile and tried to relax. "Is it really that bad? They're your family, after all."

Helen rattled the ice in her glass. Only a few flecks of golden liquid remained. "I guess I'm just not sure of my welcome. My father kicked me out, remember, once he'd caught me in the midst of perverse acts."

"But that was so long ago, Helen. I don't know, it just seems to me that with a death in the family you might be able to come together." Frieda picked up her fork and poked at the limp crust of her slice of apple pie. "It's a shame."

"Yes." Helen nodded, still staring at the blur of faces wandering back and forth in the dismal gray light. Her mind drifted back to yesterday morning, when the call from Aunt Edna had shattered the three a.m. darkness. Helen had managed to disengage herself from Frieda's embrace, grope for the phone, and croak out a hoarse greeting.

"Helen Black? Is that you?" The drawl that had always managed to sound both shrill and lazy at the same time had pierced with painful clarity through the fog sheltering Helen's consciousness. There was no mistaking who it was.

"Aunt Edna." She sighed. Frieda stirred beside her, half roused from sleep. Helen cleared her throat and tried to speak softly in spite of the knot forming in her stomach. "How are you? How's Uncle Loy? Is everything okay?"

"Well, honey —" A brief discussion ensued in which Edna shushed someone with urgent whispers. "Hon, I know it's awful early out there —"

Three-fifteen, Helen noted. "What's wrong?"

Her aunt sighed loudly. "It's your Great-aunt Ruth, hon. You know she's been sick for so long."

Helen suddenly felt cold. She drew herself up, rigid, as Frieda sat up next to her. "When did it happen?"

"Well, she died in her sleep last night. Now, I know it's been an awful long time since you've seen her, but I wanted to be the one to tell you."

Helen was lost to her aunt's ramblings as she was thrust back into memory. Great-aunt Ruth McCormick, her grandfather's sister, had been a silent, forbidding presence throughout Helen's childhood. Tightly permed steel-colored hair, features sharp as a knife, grim, thin lips tensed below cold dark eyes — Ruth inspired fear and awe. Helen was surprised at her own sense of shock. Perhaps she'd always assumed that Aunt Ruth would resist mortality, just as she'd successfully resisted husbands, childbearing and domestic duties.

Frieda was now fully awake. She reached for Helen in concern but didn't speak. With her touch Helen was pulled back into the present and to her Aunt Edna's voice. "So I thought you'd better come out to look at the house and decide what you want to do with it."

"What was that?"

"The old McCormick house. Outside Vicksburg. You remember it." She made it a statement, not a question. And of course Helen remembered it well — built by her grandfather just after she was born. The five small rooms had seemed like a mansion to her then, with their polished oak floors, the whole place shaded by magnolias and fig trees. Helen could practically taste the sweet pulp of the figs now, the memory preserved just like fruit in thick syrup.

"None of us knew what she would do with it. It's falling all apart now — what? Oh, hush, Loy. That's your uncle saying he thinks you should sell it."

Realization sank in. "Wait a minute. That house is mine now?"

"Spiegel Morris — you remember him, your mother's second cousin from Tupelo? The one who married Alice. Well, anyhow, he was Ruth's lawyer, and they took out the will after she went into the hospital last time." Slowly it came out, with prompting from Uncle Loy in the background. The house, uninhabited for at least a decade, now belonged to her. Whether she wanted it or not.

"But — but why did she leave it to me?"

Silence on the other end. "Hon, I really think you ought to come on out here. Her funeral is in two days, at the old Bethel church. Everybody will be there."

Helen felt as if a huge stone were sinking inside her. Slowly she reached for the bedside lamp, then picked up the pen and pad next to the phone. Frieda rubbed her eyes and continued to watch in sympathetic silence while Helen jotted down the information. "I'll have to see if I can get a flight, and a hotel —"

"Now you just get into Memphis and Loy will come get you. Won't you, Loy? You can stay out here with us in Corinth, and we'll drive to Vicksburg in the truck." Edna's repeated assurances didn't ease Helen's mind as she reluctantly agreed to try to get to Mississippi in time to bury Ruth McCormick. Anyway, she was too astonished by it all to protest. Besides —

"Hey." Helen turned back to Frieda, who gazed at her with an odd expression. "Where are you?"

In answer, Helen pulled her wallet from an overstuffed carry-on bag and fished out a photograph. She studied it for a moment, fingering the creases and tattered edges, before handing it to Frieda. "Meet Edna and Loy McCormick."

"Who's the other one? The younger guy standing behind them."

Helen could see the images clearly in her mind, fixed there by years of familiarity. It was the only family photograph she'd kept. "That's their only son, Bob. They call him Junior, but don't ask me why. He is, as my mother used to say, 'a bit lacking.' He had spinal meningitis as a little kid."

"How old is he?"

"Probably about forty now." Helen watched her lover, wondering how Frieda saw her relatives — Edna's flowered "Sunday-go-to-meeting" dress stretched tight across her wide hips, her plump white face framed by cat's-eye glasses and tightly permed hair; Uncle Loy with his perennial baseball cap advertising John Deere farm equipment, his baggy blue Sears suit hanging on his skinny frame; and her cousin Bob, who very slightly resembled Helen in his steady brown eyes and square face, vacantly grinning at the camera as he towered over his parents. In the background was the old pickup, dinged and dented from many years of hard service while Uncle Loy drove back and forth across Mississippi supplementing his meager income from farming by repairing tractors and other machinery. Helen remembered taking the picture the day of her graduation from high school. She could still feel the warmth of the June sun on her shoulders, still hear herself telling the trio to say "cheese" as she pushed the button on the camera, still see them frozen in awkward tableau in the front yard of their home in Corinth.

Frieda handed her the picture. "They look like nice people, Helen," she said softly, a hint of sadness in her voice. "Too bad it's been so long since you saw them."

Helen hid her face from Frieda as she slid the photograph back into her wallet. "Well, it just seemed the best way. When my father kicked me out, I was so hurt and scared. I wanted to run and keep on running and never look back."

They sat in silence for a moment. Frieda sighed and pushed her plate away from her. "I don't know why I ordered this," she said. "Airport food is always terrible."

"Not to mention expensive," Helen responded as she picked up the check. "I was going to buy something to read in the bookstore, but maybe I'll just save the money for a couple of drinks on the plane."

"Oh, that reminds me! I almost forgot this." Frieda leaned down and reached for something on the floor. "While you were checking your bags I went to the newsstand. You'll never believe what I saw there."

Helen looked down in amazement at the copy of

the Warren County *Ledger* Frieda placed in her hands. "You're right—I can't believe it. Why on earth would they carry this newspaper here?"

Frieda shrugged. "Well, they have newspapers from all over the world. I asked the cashier if they had anything from Mississippi, and he found this. Maybe it's an omen. Vicksburg is in this county, right?"

"Right." Ten slim pages told the news of Vicksburg and the surrounding towns. Helen glanced at the date. "This is from last week. Guess there won't be anything about Aunt Ruth here."

A voice loudly announced that Helen's flight to Memphis was now boarding. Frieda snatched the check. "No, it's my turn," she said as they walked to the cashier. Helen followed her out and they made their way through the thin stream of people toward the gate.

"Helen, are you sure you don't want me to go with you?" Frieda asked as Helen found her boarding pass.

Helen shook her head. They'd already talked about this. "I just don't know what kind of welcome I'm going to get, Frieda. Besides, you have that exhibit down in Los Angeles this weekend. You don't want to miss that."

Frieda grimaced. "I think that the great Frieda Lawrence, artiste extraordinaire, could stand to miss one exhibit."

"But Helen Black, the amazing hard-boiled private eye, would not want that to happen." Helen smiled, then swiftly reached out to hug Frieda. "I'll call you as soon as I get there." As she approached the boarding ramp, she turned back for one last look at

Frieda, a small forlorn figure that waved at her then disappeared from view.

Helen walked slowly down the ramp, taking the newspaper out as she waited her turn to greet the smiling flight attendants and find her seat. Better to find something to focus on besides Freida's sad face. Just before she was accosted by the nearest attendant, she read the headline on page one, its huge black letters announcing the grim news:

SECOND BODY OF YOUNG BLACK WOMAN FOUND NEAR RIVER. SERIAL KILLER STALKS WARREN COUNTY.

Chapter Two

It might have been the same truck in the photograph Helen had shown Frieda — same beat-up green American model, creaking and groaning down the state highway from Memphis to Corinth. In the dreamlike state induced by the airline's bourbon, Helen stared out the window into the darkness that was broken only by the yellow headlights of Uncle Loy's truck. A few wisps of white gauzy cotton, relics of the harvest going on farther west, toward the rich silt of the Delta, floated on the late September breeze across Helen's line of vision. Now and then the hulks of farm machinery emerged in the fields like prehistoric beasts jarred from the sleep of eons by the truck's rattling progress across northern Mississippi.

Helen found herself staring at her own reflection in the window, her face illuminated by the greenish glow from the dashboard. Of course, the hours of travel, lack of sleep, and anxiety over seeing her family after a hiatus of almost fifteen years didn't help her appearance. With growing distaste she observed her pale bony face, the heavy squared features looking pasty against the black night. Only her eyes were alive, dark and deep-set above the high cheekbones that her mother always swore came from Cherokee blood. She grimaced, ran a hand through her short hair in an effort to stay awake.

Next to her own reflection she saw Uncle Loy's image as he peered through the windshield, hunched over the steering wheel. With a surge of pleasure she couldn't explain, she turned to look at him. She'd had no trouble recognizing him at the Memphis airport. Same cheap faded denim, same John Deere cap. Only the glasses were different — thicker lenses told the passage of time.

"How's Bob doing?" she asked.

Loy cleared his throat. " 'Bout the same. Still goin' to the center in Jackson twice a week for classes and such. Edna takes him down when she gets her hair done." Helen saw his crooked grin surface. "He was all excited when he knew you was coming."

In that smile and that comment was all the affection she had sensed when he'd given her a brief, fierce hug at the airport, and she felt relieved and even happy. Words had never been necessary to Uncle Loy, she knew. It was enough for him to be near those he loved, to do things for them.

"It'll be nice to see him. I'm surprised he remembers me."

"He talks about fishin' with you. Remember how y'all used to go out to Perry's Creek on Saturdays?"

"He always brought home a lot more than I did."

Flashing lights ahead cut reverie short. Helen felt Uncle Loy tense as they passed the highway patrolman who was writing up a ticket at the window of a souped-up Corvette, the driver slumped disconsolate at the steering wheel, his pimpled face and thin frame revealing his youth and fear. Loy visibly relaxed as the red and blue lamps receded behind them. What was he so nervous about?

"Mississippi's finest on the job," she said with a small laugh, hoping to dispel the anxiety.

"Hope so."

Triggered by the sight of uniformed authority, Helen recalled the newspaper headlines. "I saw something about a series of murders near Vicksburg. What's that all about?"

Again he tensed. The small round face drew in on itself and he hunched closer to the steering wheel, one hand nervously stroking the gearshift. "Found a coupla young colored girls out in that patch near the Big Black, where it gets close to Yokena. South of Vicksburg."

Helen watched how his knuckles whitened on the gearshift. "The *Ledger* says they — they were pretty messed up," she said, groping for a euphemism for rape and mutilation.

He pursed his lips, raised a hand to the

dashboard for the package of cigarettes resting there. "Some nut, they think. Maybe one got loose from the state hospital in Jackson." The dashboard lighter glowed red near his face and a thin stream of gray-blue smoke clouded the air between them.

Helen breathed in the scent of a Camel. She hadn't smoked in years. "Can I have one of those?" He handed her the package, and a moment later she was savoring the long-forgotten heady feel of a good cigarette. Suddenly the tiredness dissipated. "You think Aunt Edna might have some leftovers in the fridge?"

He chuckled. "I don't know where you put it all. You still must have that hollow leg. I think I saw some fried chicken and coleslaw in there. Maybe some peach cobbler, if Bob didn't eat it all this afternoon."

"It'll be a nice change." She sighed after taking another long, deep drag. "Most places I go to eat have lots of bean sprouts and tofu."

His face crinkled in confusion. "What the hell is tofu?"

She relaxed further into the seat. "Don't ask. No fat, no salt, no cholesterol."

"No damn good." They laughed together.

Helen considered bringing up the subject of the murders again, then decided against it. She'd do a little snooping around on her own while she was here, and then — no. She had no business sticking her nose in this. She was here to see her family, and that was that. She suddenly felt a pang when she thought of Frieda, who had been her only family for years.

He broke into her thoughts. "Any of this look familiar?"

"My God." She stared in amazement at the small cluster of buildings they were passing. "Nothing has changed at all." There was Dan's Bait and Tackle, and right next to it the rickety wooden frame where the Johnson brothers had sold fresh produce. Helen recalled how everyone, regardless of skin color, had frequented both establishments, despite the fact that the Johnsons had descended from slaves who'd worked the big plantations south of Vicksburg. "Are the Johnsons still here?" she asked as the truck wheezed up the grade bypassing the town of Corinth.

"Tom's grandson takes care of this on weekends, with his grandmother. Tom died last year."

Helen turned away, saddened. "Too bad. He was a nice man."

Next was the Kingdom of God chapel. The tiny building still sported incongruous Gothic columns on its nondescript squat structure. Although she couldn't see it in the dark, Helen was positive the baseball diamond remained carved in the grass behind the church. In her day she'd slammed a few home runs into the kudzu patch behind the fence, making her despised by the girls and envied by the boys.

Now her uncle changed gears, and they were approaching the gravel lane that led to his house south of Corinth. A marker stood ramrod straight in a small cleared patch, its ornate red borders noting that this site had been a rallying point for General Nathan Bedford Forrest and his cavalry on their way north to the bloodbath of Shiloh.

Helen sighed and closed her eyes. She couldn't understand why memory was so painful. Hadn't she left all this behind a long time ago? She was another person now — a successful private investigator, living on the other side of the country, with a happy, well-established home and a beautiful woman as a lover. The person she was now had nothing to do with the gawky kid who'd never belonged anywhere.

She opened her eyes and stared ahead stoically, ahead into the distance where Edna and Loy had lived for years. Uncle Loy's attention was fixed on the road ahead as they crunched and bumped down the lane, but she knew he'd been watching her, probably worrying about her.

"I might have been here only yesterday," she said with forced cheerfulness.

"Well —" He switched gears as they passed the Wilsons' house, its elaborate garden stuffed with elves and trolls and cute little bunnies. "Sometimes that's good, and sometimes that's bad, ain't it?"

"I guess I'm about to find that out." They slowed in front of a converted trailer Loy and Edna had placed in a small clearing when Helen was a toddler. The headlights flashed onto a small round woman clad in a faded housedress. With folded hands, she was waiting on the narrow front porch. Helen had thought she'd be nervous at seeing Aunt Edna, but all her fears vanished as the woman trotted across the lawn and reached her short arms around Helen's body in a tight hug. Helen thought she heard Edna sniffle as she returned the hug.

"My Lord, my Lord! I'd've known you anywhere!"

Helen started to respond, then simply held on tight as emotion clouded her eyes and clogged her throat. Loy stood in the background holding Helen's suitcase.

It was Edna who pulled away first, wiping her eyes. "Darlin', you look so pretty!"

Helen laughed. "You never could tell a lie, Aunt Edna."

"She's been talkin' about fried chicken since she set foot on the ground." Loy chuckled and squeezed past the women into the house.

Edna wrung her tiny, plump hands and pursed her lips. "Well, now, there's a little problem there."

Loy set down the suitcase with a thump. "Did y'all eat everything already? Shoot, there was enough to feed Sherman's army in that kitchen!"

"It's Bob, sweetheart. He's — he's gone off and done it again." She followed her husband up the steps, Helen close behind. As soon as she entered the trailer, Helen remembered. Sure enough, the gun rack mounted on the cheap, shiny plywood paneling was empty. Loy sighed, slapped his cap against his thigh. Helen put her arm around Edna's shoulders.

"So he's still pawning your guns to buy train tickets?" she asked.

Loy shook his head and turned to look at them. "I guess he just got so excited about you coming here, he couldn't help himself. You remember Ed Moss? Has the Dixie Pawn Shop, just outside Tupelo? Bob takes those old shotguns over to Ed, and Ed gives him a coupla bucks before he gives me a call. Bob still can't get it through his head that no trains been running from that old Tupelo station for years and years. That's where I always find him, waiting by the tracks."

Edna leaned into Helen's shoulder. "Ed called right after you left. I didn't even see Bobby go off, I was so busy talking to Fran Wilson next door —" She broke off into sobs.

Helen patted Edna's back, watching her uncle. Bob had been doing this for years, she knew. Why was everyone so upset about it now? Loy refused to meet her gaze.

"Guess I'd better go get him," he mumbled as he stomped past the women. "I reckon my guns will be safe with Ed for the night."

"I'll go with you, Uncle Loy." Helen could see that her aunt was fighting off tears. It might be easier for Edna to have a few minutes alone to calm down. "It's not that far to Tupelo. Don't worry — my stomach can handle another half-hour without your fried chicken."

"Well, if you're sure." She trailed them back to the porch and watched while Loy revved up the motor and backed out onto the gravel.

The brief ride to Tupelo was quiet. Once or twice Helen started to ask a question, but she stopped after seeing Loy's face. They proceeded without a word until they reached the outskirts of Tupelo.

The peace and darkness was broken suddenly by the flashing red and blue lights of the law. Clumps of people lined the main highway, and Uncle Loy slowed down to avoid hitting them.

"Dang fools," he spat out through rigid lips. It was a strong statement, coming from him, and Helen watched him uneasily. "There's Billy Wallace." He edged the truck over onto the shoulder. "Maybe he knows what on earth is going on out here."

Helen peered ahead as she waited in the truck. Both local police and highway patrol were here. Must be something pretty big. Yellow tape fluttered in the faint breeze, its limp motion somehow threatening with its association from Helen's past as a police officer.

Loy opened the door and slid into the cab. Even in the dim light Helen could make out his gray, drawn face. "They found another one."

Chapter Three

Wedged tight between Uncle Loy and Aunt Edna in the pickup, headed for the funeral in Vicksburg, Helen briefly looked behind her as they backed out onto the gravel road. Bob stood there, amidst the bunnies and trolls and sunflowers in Fran Wilson's garden, waving good-bye with a huge grin spread over his vacant features, his beefy body ill-fitting a man whose mental capacities had frozen at age nine. It was a completely different Bob from the one Loy and Helen had found last night. Then he'd been quivering and fearful, wandering around the fringes of the crowd that had gathered in ghoulish expectation of excitement.

"I saw her, I saw her," he'd murmured as he huddled next to his father. In his terror, tearful and moaning, he'd barely noticed Helen's presence, clinging instead to his father with big grimy hands. "They kilt her, Daddy, they cut her all up."

That tight, gray look had crept over Loy's face, and Helen knew better than to break her own silence.

The look was still there as they turned off the gravel road onto Highway 45 leading south. It struck Helen that they had almost three hours of driving ahead. Since living in Berkeley, she'd grown accustomed to darting in and out of narrow city streets. The huge, hot expanse of road, already shimmering from the morning sun, stretched out like a black snake before them. Nothing was close to anything else in Mississippi. Helen tried to relax and focus her mind on something besides the rising temperature and the humidity.

Suddenly Edna let out a sob in a ragged burst. "I don't care, Loy." She sniffled. One plump hand dabbed at her rouged cheeks as she stammered, "I think we ought to tell her."

"Now, Edna, you promised —"

"But she's a detective! She can get to the bottom of all this." She reached out and took hold of Helen's hand with a fierce clutch that belied her own soft, doughy appearance. Loy sighed and scratched his head, which was beaded with sweat. Edna stared straight ahead as the whole story spilled out.

With the first murder, they hadn't paid much attention to the fact that Bob had disappeared for several hours that night. "We was worried, but usually he'd turn up with one of the neighbors. He never could remember to call us, you know," Edna said. They'd put his disheveled appearance and strange silence down to just another one of his "moods."

It was not until the discovery of the second body that things began to add up.

Edna shook her head and closed her eyes. "He walked in the door just after midnight, his clothes sopping wet and all muddy. He kept talking about people — someone — being dead and how he'd seen it. Then the next day the news about the second body was on the radio."

"That would have been last week," Helen said, remembering the newspaper. "But really, I can't imagine Bob doing a thing like that! He's the gentlest man alive! I've never even seen him kill a bug. Besides, how would he get out as far as Vicksburg?"

"That's it, Helen," Loy said, speaking for the first time. "Maybe some gang or other is getting him mixed up in all this. He'd never do anything like this on his own."

Helen could think of nothing less likely than her poor cousin Bob playing the role of violent killer in a roving band of marauders. "I think it has to be coincidence. Something scared him, maybe stories about the deaths —"

"Then what was he doing last night out by

Tupelo walking around in the dark?" Loy shook his head. "And that's not the worst thing, not by a long shot."

Helen waited while Loy and Edna exchanged glances. Now what misery were they going to reveal?

Edna leaned forward and rummaged underneath the floor mat. She pulled out a gleaming hunting knife with an ebony handle. Helen removed it from its leather sheath. She remembered it well from her childhood, when Uncle Loy had cleaned fish and small game caught during their trips out in the woods by Perry's Creek. He would never let her touch its thick, smooth metal, but she used to watch him in silent admiration, longing to be part of the male world of hunting and fishing and handling such beautiful deadly instruments.

"We're keeping it locked up out here now, since Bob can get into anything he wants to in the house." Edna wiped her eyes, watching Helen touch the blade. "He had it in his pocket last week when he showed up that night, all over blood and dirt."

"But what did he say? I mean, he must have had some explanation of how he got it."

"I tried to ask him, but he just pitched a fit when he looked at it, yellin' and cryin', fit to be tied." Edna looked away as Helen replaced the knife in the worn leather case. "So I just cleaned it up and now we keep it locked in the truck."

"I keep the keys so he can't ever get in here," Loy added. With an abrupt motion he reached across Helen's lap and patted his wife on the hand. "Honey, we just don't know what this is all about," he said to

Edna. "I really don't think it's fair to drag Helen in on this."

"She's family." Helen knew that firm voice, that jutting of double chins. Edna wiped away her tears. "Helen, you were always like a daughter to us, and you still are. I ain't sayin' nothin' about how you live your life, as long as you're happy. But you're the only sister Bob will ever have, and I know you'll want to help us."

The cab of the truck was already getting hot as the sun climbed higher. Helen writhed inwardly as she mulled over her aunt's words. She never should have stepped onto that plane. Whoever had said you can't go home again was dead right. Edna patted her hand, and Helen felt guilt creeping over her once again. How could she refuse to help them? Not after what they'd done for her fifteen years ago.

With a sigh she said, "I'll talk to Bob. Maybe he'll tell me something about what happened to him those nights. I still think there's no way on earth he could have done such things, or be involved with them in any way."

Her uncle fidgeted next to her. Helen shot him a glance, taking in his blank stare. Edna, too, was looking straight ahead, her round face as still as stone. The couple exchanged looks over her, and Helen knew there was something else. She suddenly felt angry.

"Is that everything you can tell me about Bob?" she asked, carefully controlling her irritation.

Edna opened her mouth, but Loy cut her off. "That's it," he said curtly. "That's all we know, hon." Edna subsided into her own world, and looked out of the window, releasing Helen's hand. Helen decided then and there to merely ask Bob some cautious questions and let it go. Surely this was all imagination on their part.

Uncle Loy turned on the radio and found a station playing country music. For over an hour they listened to the moanings of various honky-tonk habitues wailing out their sodden despair, the songs interspersed with blaring advertisements. Distracted by her own thoughts, Helen barely heard any of it. Before she knew it they were on Highway 20 heading west from Jackson. Jerked back to the present by the familiar landscape, Helen's stomach tightened in anxiety. How many times, as a teenager, had she driven along this same road in late-night jaunts to Jackson, in search of any excitement that might alleviate the misery at home? The highway followed the old train tracks, and she remembered stories of how Grant's boys in blue had tramped across these hills on their way to Vicksburg. As they passed Bolton and Champion's Hill, Helen thought of her grandfather, who used to regale them with tales of the glorious Confederate past.

"How's Granddaddy?" she asked. "There was so much going on last night I forgot to ask about everyone."

Aunt Edna seemed relieved to be talking about something other than her son. "Oh, honey, I guess no one told you. He's been in the hospital for a few months. We won't see him today."

"What happened?"

"Stroke," her uncle replied as he downshifted. The truck slowed and traffic grew heavier. They were on the outskirts of the National Military Park now. Helen felt cold, in spite of the smothering heat that soaked down to the bone. Yes, here was the old road that led to the Bethel Baptist Church. The red clouds of dust that used to billow behind them as they drove to church each Sunday were a thing of the past — the road had been paved, and the truck sped along smoothly over the asphalt. Through the sparse clumps of thin pine Helen could see the gray and white humps of markers in the cemetery, where generations of Blacks and McCormicks had been buried since the early eighteenth century.

The truck groaned to a halt a few yards from the entrance of the plain, squat brick building, its exterior gleaming with repeated applications of whitewash. Helen felt herself sweating in her black linen suit, and her ankles wobbled, unaccustomed to the spike heels, as she and Edna and Loy made their procession across the inevitable gravel walk. Silence fell over the knots of whispering mourners who turned to stare at the sexual pervert from the evil realms of San Francisco. Edna took her hand and jutted her plump chin as she nodded a greeting to several women. Loy followed close behind, like a rear guard protecting the flanks.

Helen took her cue from Edna and defiantly said hello to some of the staring faces. What the hell, she thought, it's all grist for the mill. With a sudden wish that Frieda were at her side she mounted the narrow steps and entered the cool darkness of the church.

Chapter Four

The vinyl-covered sofa creaked beneath the weight of the four adults sitting on it. Helen furtively surveyed the faces of her relatives gathered in Cousin Hal Black's living room. The scent of simmering pot roast wafted over their heads while Cousin Spiegel Morris, the lawyer who'd attended to Aunt Ruth's final wishes, sorted papers with deft, finicky fingers at the old scratched dining room table that Cousin Maud, Hal's wife, had tried in vain to keep polished and unblemished through years of children and meals and general abuse. Maud herself stepped out from the kitchen, wiping her hands on the faded print apron with dingy ruffles that covered her blue church dress. While Spiegel cleared his throat and adjusted his glasses, Helen, watching Maud, remembered how a couple of hours ago her cousin had blushed and looked terribly embarrassed at Helen's friendly greeting.

"Edna thought you might be coming," Maud had whispered as Helen and her aunt and uncle, amid the curious stares, slid into a pew near the center of the church. The vibrating tones of the organ had covered their procession to the front of the church where the trio gazed in silence into the polished coffin, at the mortal remains of Ruth McCormick. Helen had felt too awkward to register the appropriate sadness at the sight of the unfamiliar figure, the sharp, grim features sunken beneath the grotesquely caked makeup. Her great-aunt had always been something of an awe-inspiring stranger to her, and Helen felt more than ever like an alien visitor as she leafed through the hymnal.

Spiegel's high-pitched whine pierced her musings. "I think," he began, "that y'all are aware of the terms of Ruth's will." Everyone squirmed in anticipation as he read aloud. "The property is divided up . . ."

Helen observed with detachment their tense faces and nervously twining hands. Aunt Louise McCormick, Ruth's half-sister, wore a tiny smile on her bright red lips, as if she were savoring some sweet morsel. She was to get the rich timberland that Ruth had been leasing to a highly profitable manufacturer. Beside her, Cousin David Garrett, another of Edna's nephews, sat stone-faced with his wife Irma. They heard the news that they had rights only to the household goods that Ruth had collected over the years. Maud, perched on the arm of Hal's easy chair, relaxed as Spiegel announced that her family would be able to stay rent- and mortgage-free in the house where they were gathered.

"And finally —" Spiegel peered up through his bifocals in disapproval as Maud and Hal's two youngest darted through the living room, giggling at their own precocity, in some indeterminate game. Maud reached out a swift hand in reprimand, but they were too fast for her. "Finally," Spiegel continued, "there's the old house out on Pemberton Road."

"Yes, we had a question about that," David said in his rumbling, deliberate tone. With a nervous glance at Helen, he twitched at the belt that fit too tight over his paunch. "I believe there was a clause that left it open to question about who was to inherit that house, wasn't there?"

Spiegel twisted his lips, irritated at the interruption. "If you'll just allow me to finish, I believe it will all be clear." He rambled on as they all sneaked a look at Helen, who was only half-listening. Let them have it, she thought. I'll never come back here again.

She didn't try to follow the legal maze that Spiegel attempted to explain to them, gathering only that she and she alone was to receive ownership of the crumbling ruin on the outskirts of Vicksburg. "She also provided a fund for repairs to the house, should Helen wish to do that."

"How much?" Aunt Louise spat out, instantly coloring with embarrassment over her spiteful tone.

Spiegel looked at Helen as if asking for permission to speak. When Helen shrugged and smiled, he told them. "It's in the area of thirty thousand, I believe. Mostly tied up in mutual funds that can easily be converted to liquid assets."

"Cold hard cash, in other words," Hal said as he gripped the armrest in a quick spasm.

"I wouldn't advise that," Spiegel said, then began another long monologue about trust funds and taxes. Nobody really listened, nor did they dare look at Helen, who was thinking that maybe she could set something up for Edna and Loy with a part of her share — once she sold the house, of course.

Spiegel looked aggrieved as he was once again interrupted, this time by a knock on the door. Maud sprang up and hurried to see who it was, while everyone else shifted in their seats or stood and stretched. At least it was all out on the table now. Even Spiegel began collecting his documents, slipping them into the gleaming leather briefcase that rested, incongruous, on the cuts and scratches of the table. Suddenly everyone froze as the intruder stepped into the living room. Like playing statues, Helen thought as she helped Edna up from the sofa. When she turned around she saw the reason for their reaction.

The woman's face was all too familiar, even though she was dressed in the official khaki of the local police. The leather belt that held the regulation pistol encircled a waist that had thickened only slightly with the passing years. Soft brown eyes looked at her from under curly blonde hair. At once Helen was transported back to her high school days, when she'd been hopelessly, painfully in love with the woman who stood before her wearing a police officer's uniform.

Hal cleared his throat and stood up. "Beth Wilks! Haven't seen you in quite a while."

She smiled and shook his hand, turning so that her smile took in the entire room. Murmurs of surprised greeting ebbed as the family members glanced at one another nervously. Helen guessed they were wondering whether or not this was an official visit.

Beth spoke as if she'd read their thoughts. "Just wanted to pay my respects." Then she met Helen's eyes, and a faint blush crept over her cheeks. "I heard you were coming back."

They shook hands. Helen felt Loy and Edna staring at them. She was sure that they were the only ones who knew that Beth Wilks was the reason her father had kicked her out and sent her away without a cent. Although the older couple had taken her in without judgment or question, Helen was certain they'd held Beth in contempt for what she'd done to their niece.

Beth dropped her hand. "I just got off duty. Thought I'd run out this way before I went home. I'm real sorry I couldn't be at the funeral this morning."

Maud fussed with her apron as her youngest girl tugged at her mother's arm. "Dinner will be ready in about half an hour, Beth," Maud said, shaking the child off. "Why don't you stay and eat with us?"

Helen knew Beth hesitated only because of her

presence. Her voice rang out in the quiet room. "Would you mind very much, Maud, if I borrowed Loy's truck and took a drive out to Pemberton Road? I'd like to see the house again."

Everyone fell silent, and Helen realized she'd blurted out the wrong thing. It made her sound grubby and greedy, as if she couldn't wait to gloat over her inheritance, when all she'd wanted to do was escape the stares and remarks of this unending day.

"Why don't I drive you out there?" Beth said. "Don't worry, Maud, we'll be back in plenty of time." She was heading for the door before Helen could protest. Helen slid past her and out onto the driveway, where the black and white patrol car waited. She sat, wordless and irritated, as Beth steered the car onto the road.

Helen didn't speak until they'd turned onto Pemberton. "You're the last person I expected to see today," she said. She caught a glimpse of Beth's crooked grin. "How did you know I was going to be here?"

"You forget what it's like out here." Beth rested one arm on the open window and steered easily with one hand. "Everybody knows everybody's business. I also know your aunt left you this house."

Helen sighed, not knowing whether to laugh or be angry. "Next thing I know you'll be telling me details of my life in California."

"You'd be surprised." Beth was quiet for a moment as they hit a few ruts in the road, then she went on. "Edna and Loy keep me posted from time to time."

"Oh, really? That's interesting. You sure didn't

give a damn about me after you went to the preacher and confessed your perversions to him — all that unnatural passion I'd inspired in you." Helen stopped abruptly when she realized how bitter she sounded.

Beth reddened and gripped the steering wheel with both hands. "Helen, we were just kids —"

"So that excuses everything."

Beth pulled off the road onto a dirt path. The overarching trees, hung with Spanish moss, threw welcome shade onto the car. Too upset with herself and with Beth to speak anymore, Helen got out before Beth had even turned off the engine.

Beth waited in the car while Helen strode around the house. She'd forgotten to get a key. Maybe it wasn't locked, she thought. But the front door rattled and withstood her attempts to open it. This was a big mistake, Helen thought as she walked around to the back door. She should come back alone tomorrow.

The back door resisted her efforts. With an angry sigh Helen surveyed the walls before her. The building sagged and tottered on the red clay soil. Part of the foundation was exposed to the elements. Helen crouched down to peer at the gray stone blocks that showed through the dirt, dismayed at the dilapidated condition of the house. It would take a long time to get it ready to sell, and even then —

Helen shuddered as a sudden chill swept over her body. She groped behind her until her hand found a loose stick. Carefully she poked and prodded at the clumps of earth that clung to the slender length of white fabric. As the soil fell away, the white fragment loosened and fell free. The shape, the length, the joint in the center — nausea gripped Helen as she realized what kind of remains she was looking at. She dropped the stick, backed away from the house and shouted for Beth.

Chapter Five

From her seat on the porch swing Helen watched as Beth spoke into the mike, telling the chief constable of their gruesome discovery. Helen's cheeks still burned with shame as she thought of how she'd acted — she'd almost thrown up when she'd told Beth to take a look at the foundation of the house. Helen had seen death in many forms during her years as a police officer in Berkeley, but somehow the fact that these remains were buried beneath Great-aunt Ruth's house added an extra element of horror to the sight of the fragile bones breaking into the red clay. The body must have been put there as the house was being built, but Helen didn't know for certain when that was. At least 1958 — or no, maybe 1959, the year that Helen, was born. Edna and Loy would know for sure, or Maud would. And did this mean that a member of her own family had been involved in the death and burial of an unidentified corpse? But the building of the McCormick house must have been common knowledge in Vicksburg. Anyone might have —

Helen put a halt to her speculations as Beth walked away from the patrol car and approached the porch. She had put her sunglasses on, and Helen couldn't make out her expression beneath the opaque lenses.

"Your aunt and uncle will be coming out here," she said, placing one booted foot on the steps as she pulled a package of cigarettes from her pocket.

Helen refused her offer of a smoke. "I guess they've figured out we won't be there for dinner." She watched as Beth took a deep drag and exhaled slowly. A few flakes of ash drifted across the porch. "Is there a team coming out here? A coroner, people to gather evidence —"

Beth turned her blank face away and stared out toward the dirt road. "Well, it may not be Berkeley, but we have conducted a few murder investigations out here in the sticks, Helen. Just like uptown."

Helen sighed. "I'm sorry, Beth. I'm just babbling. I can't seem to take in the fact that my aunt has been living here for years, while all the time . . ." Helen let her words trail off. The afternoon sun glared across the porch, and she felt sick again. She'd forgotten what this heat was like. It drenched her body, sinking into her bones, all energy drained in the effort to be still and quiet.

Beth sat down on the steps, her eyes fixed on the road. "How old is this house, Helen?"

Helen opened her eyes. She noticed that sweat beaded Beth's forehead above her sunglasses. "I think it was built the year I was born, nineteen fifty-nine. Uncle Loy will know for sure."

Beth ground her cigarette beneath her boot. "Your grandfather built it himself, right?"

"That's right. I mean, he must have had different people helping him out, you know. So everyone in town had to know that he was doing it." Helen stopped when she heard how lame she sounded. Of course Beth had to ask these questions. She shouldn't take it so personally.

Beth removed her sunglasses and wiped her forehead with a handkerchief. "I'm sure the whole town knew. Robert McCormick was a highly respected citizen — chief constable, his grandfather a hero at Shiloh, lots of land and lots of money."

"Not to mention that he was more than likely a card-carrying member of the local KKK chapter."

"Is that true, Helen?"

Helen looked away, shifting on the porch swing. "I don't know, really. Guess I'm making assumptions again."

"I was sorry to hear he's in the hospital. How bad is it?"

Helen was surprised at the lump in her throat. "He probably has only a few weeks left. We — Uncle Loy and Aunt Edna were going to take me over to see him tonight."

"Think I could go with you?"

Helen looked up in surprise. Surely this wasn't a social call. Perhaps Beth was hoping she could find out something about the building of the house. "Sure, if you want to. I don't know if he'll even know we're in the room, though."

Beth's response was cut off by the arrival of several cars, their presence announced by the enormous clouds of dust visible over the trees as they sped down the dirt road. An ambulance and two more patrol cars, followed by a station wagon with the state seal emblazoned on the side, lined up in front of Ruth McCormick's house. Edna and Loy brought up the rear, the pickup groaning to a halt at the edge of the overgrown lawn. Helen felt a sudden surge of emotion at the sight of the elderly couple clambering out of the vehicle and nervously picking their way across the kudzu that threatened to conquer the yard.

"Darlin'!" Edna reached up to give her niece a hug as Helen rose from the porch swing. "I just can't believe all this is happening," she murmured in a tremulous voice.

Loy hovered nearby, twisting his cap in his hands, his gaze darting across the people swarming toward the back of the house. Helen focused on Beth as she spoke briefly to two uniformed men. They glanced at the group standing on the porch, then silently went to join the others. Beth walked back to where Helen stood. Helen tried to read her countenance again, but it was still a blank.

"Why don't y'all go on in the house? It's gettin' pretty hot out here. We'll try not to keep you too long."

Loy fished a key from his pocket. "I got this from

Maud." He glanced at Beth and the other officers grouped on the lawn before fumbling with the lock.

Helen felt dizzy as they stepped into the dim, musty house. It was only slightly cooler inside, but at least they'd be out of the sun. The screen door slammed, leaving Beth outside watching them as she lit another cigarette. Helen stood uncertainly in the middle of the foyer. To her surprise, she was able to recall precisely how everything in the house was situated — she made her way across the living room without bumping into a single chair or table or doorway. The lamp next to the sofa stayed dark when Helen turned the switch, but dim sunlight filtered in through the grime on the windows.

"I wonder if I can rustle up a glass of water." Helen headed for the kitchen, her feet striking against the wooden floor that still gleamed beneath a layer of dust. She was relieved to see how clean the kitchen was. Water sputtered, a rusty brown, out of the ancient faucet. Helen let it run until it flowed clear, rinsed out one of Aunt Ruth's crystal glasses, then stood at the sink and stared at the bands of sunlight forcing their way through the shutters. Helen set the glass down and threw open the shutters. Warmth flooded the small room, and she saw Beth conferring with her colleagues on the lawn just below. Beth stood up at the sound of the shutters swinging open, while the two men with her remained bent over the corner of the house, just outside the kitchen, where Helen had seen the bones. Beth moved away from the others, heading for the back door that led into the kitchen. Helen went to meet her. She saw Beth level her gaze on the glass in her hand.

"I was just getting Aunt Edna a glass of water. Sorry, I should have asked you first if I could touch anything in the house."

Beth shrugged and removed her sunglasses. Helen looked away, startled at the effect Beth's eyes had on her. She had forgotten how intense they were.

"It's okay," Beth said. "Any evidence inside the house is long gone."

"Do they have any idea when the body was put there?"

Beth didn't answer immediately. Of course, Helen realized, she's wondering how much she can tell me. When Beth finally spoke she chose her words with care. "Well, at least since the house was built. That's, what, thirty-five years now? Looks like the storms we've had the last couple of years, as well as the age of the house, washed away enough of the land to expose the foundation."

Helen drank the water in one gulp, then moved to the sink to fill it again. "Whoever put the foundation in didn't do a very good job."

"Maybe they were in a hurry."

Suddenly dizzy, Helen set the glass down on the sideboard, hoping that her hand wasn't visibly trembling. She felt Beth come up behind her.

"You okay, Helen?" Her hands rested for a moment on Helen's shoulders, and without thinking Helen let herself lean back, feeling Beth's body strong and firm against her. They sprang apart as if they'd both been subjected to an electrical shock.

Helen gripped the glass and managed to produce a chuckle. "I'm not used to this weather anymore. And I haven't eaten in a while."

"That's what living in California does — makes

you soft." Beth remained where she was, her hands at her sides. "Maybe you'd better take that to Edna."

"Right." Beth followed her through the baize door. Loy stood up as they entered. "Here you are, Aunt Edna."

The older woman drank steadily, draining the glass with thirsty gulps. "Thank you, sweetheart," she whispered as she twisted the glass around in her hands. "I just can't seem to — I can't —"

"It's all right." Beth sat down next to her. "This has been a really terrible day for you, I know."

"Well —" Edna sighed and took a deep breath. "I know there's a lot of questions you want to ask us, but I just don't know for sure if we can help." She looked helplessly at her husband, who was nodding vigorously in agreement.

Helen watched Beth's face. There was an expression of deep sympathy on her features, but the eyes were sharp, taking in as much as possible.

"Well, I think the best thing right now is if we just let the police do their jobs. Why don't we go on to the hospital and see if we can't visit Mr. McCormick for a few minutes?"

Helen watched her aunt and uncle closely, but they showed no response to Beth's use of "we." Perhaps they saw it as a friendly gesture instead of a desire to talk to the old man.

Loy cleared his throat. "It's a long drive back home. I was just thinking —" He looked at his wife. Exhaustion lined Edna's pale sweaty face.

Beth stood up. "I could take Helen over to the hospital right now. Let's just leave that key for the boys to use."

They trooped out after Beth. Helen had no doubt

that Beth, as she gave the key to one of the men who'd been examining the house's foundation, was giving him a few hints about looking through the house.

Helen slid onto the seat and took one last look at the gathering of official vehicles on Aunt Ruth's front lawn. The flashing lights recalled the drive to Tupelo the previous night.

"Does this remind you of something more current?" Helen asked.

Beth looked at her sharply as she navigated the gravel road. "I'm surprised you heard anything about that out in California."

The interest in Beth's voice warned Helen. Beth probably had no idea, at this point, that her cousin Bob had been in Tupelo last night. Now was not the time to talk about some homicidal maniac who was romping through the state of Mississippi.

Helen folded her arms and relaxed as the air conditioner blew cool drafts over her. "I only know what I read in the papers, Beth." They were both silent as the car reached the main road, leaving dust and rocks behind on their journey to the hospital.

Chapter Six

Helen cradled the receiver of the pay phone on her shoulder as she looked down the hospital corridor. She leaned against the wall. God, she was tired — heat and emotion and exhaustion had finally won the battle. Glancing up, she saw the nurses at the station in the center of the hall, whispering and looking at her. Beth sat on one of the plastic-covered chairs nearby, arms folded across her chest, gazing at the floor. Helen turned away and gave her full attention to Frieda's voice.

"I really think I should be there with you, Helen. This is too much for you to deal with alone."

"Sweetheart, I'm fine. I'm just dead tired. How's the show going?"

"Okay, I guess. You know how it is lately — lesbians are fashionable right now. I'm taking advantage of it while I can. But are you sure I can't come out there with you? I hate to think of you all by yourself in the middle of this."

"Honey, I love you and I miss you. I'd like nothing better than to have you here. But it would just complicate things even more than they are already. And believe me, I want to get out of here as soon as possible." She heard Beth shift in her chair and wondered how much of this she'd overheard.

Frieda sighed deeply, and Helen could well imagine the exasperation her lover had on her face right now. "All right, Helen. Promise me you'll call me in the morning?"

Helen hung up after a swift reassurance and good-bye. Beth stood up as soon as Helen left the phone. "Ready?" she asked, her face still a blank. The nurses fell silent as they passed the station and went to her grandfather's room.

The bed next to the door lay empty, bare, its plain white mattress stripped, waiting for the next patient. Helen moved to the bed by the window, her heart pounding, filled with a mixture of emotions she didn't care to examine. Late afternoon sun illuminated a low table that bore an assortment of offerings — a vase filled with white and yellow chrysanthemums, a miniature evergreen in a wicker basket, a small bowl of grapes. A folding frame held two photographs. Not quite ready to look at the man lying on the bed, Helen picked it up. Both pictures were familiar. In one, taken just after World War II, her grandparents stared solemnly into the camera, as if weighed down by the terrible sobriety of the life they would share together. This photograph was paired with one taken about 1962, Helen thought. Posing in uniform, Sheriff McCormick stood in the midst of several other police officers. In the background was a smoking barbecue pit. It was one of Helen's earliest memories, and she could still hear the sizzle of roasting pork, feel herself dandled on the knees of the officers' wives. The men faced the camera proudly, except for Sheriff McCormick. The stern lines of the earlier portrait had softened to something akin to sadness.

"What's that they've got on their hats? The ribbons." Beth's voice sounded soft in her ear. With a start Helen realized how close Beth stood behind her. She set the frame down and backed away from the table.

"I don't know. They always had different colored ribbons on their hats. Not exactly regulation, I guess."

"Something like a membership badge in the good ol' boys' club." The edge of bitterness in Beth's voice made Helen wonder what Beth had had to deal with from her fellow officers. Helen was prevented from responding by a sudden movement on the bed behind them.

His eyes were open. At first he stared vaguely out into the room, slowly taking in the tubes and machinery that the hospital had erected as a barrier against death. Then he shifted his attention to the women standing before him. In her mind, Helen still carried the younger image of him represented by the framed photographs on the table. As she studied the emaciated gray figure lying on the bed, the table by the window suddenly seemed like a shrine to someone already dead. She reached out and took his hand in her own with a gentle, tentative pressure on the bony fingers.

"Hey," she whispered, fighting back tears. "I can't believe they've managed to lock you up in here. What's Warren County coming to?"

"Gone to hell in a handbasket." His voice rasped as he forced breath into his body. His eyes shone with some unintelligible emotion. "They told me my doll-baby would be here, but I didn't believe 'em."

"See? I'm just as stubborn as you are, Grandpa."

"That's the McCormick in you. Always were stubborn old cusses." He moved his head and looked at Beth standing back by the window. "Is that Beth Wilks?"

She moved closer, smiling with genuine affection. "One and the same, boss."

"Hell, I ain't been your boss for a long time now. Thought you'd be running the show, tellin' us old fellas how to do things."

Beth chuckled. "I could still use a few lessons from you."

A smile cracked his parched lips. Helen poured a glass of water from the jug on the low table by his side, but he refused her offer. "Leakin' like a sieve this days. Maybe in a minute." He fumbled with the small unit that controlled the bed's position until he'd maneuvered into a sitting posture. "Now I can see you gals." Helen was relieved to hear his voice clearing, his eyes steady.

"Funeral was today, wasn't it?"

"That's right, Grandpa."

A deep sigh sounded from the bed. "I always figured Ruth would outlast me, somehow." He shut his eyes for a moment, then snapped them open, looking past Helen at Beth. "Beth, I don't believe you're here just to pay respects to the dead and the dying."

Helen glanced back at Beth, whose cheeks had turned pink. She was surprised to see Beth so embarrassed. "It's nothing that can't wait until you're feeling better, sir."

Something resembling a laugh shook the old man beneath the sheets. "Take a good look, young lady. I don't believe I'm going to be feeling better. Not in this life, anyway." His eyes shifted back to Helen. "Darlin', we'd better put off visiting for a bit while I find out what this woman wants from an old man."

Beth and Helen glanced at each other, and Helen decided to start. "Grandpa, we went out to Aunt Ruth's house today —"

"Out on Pemberton, off the highway?" He suddenly became very still, and an unreadable expression crept over his wasted features. "She left that to you in her will."

"Well, I just thought I'd take a look at it, see how much it needed fixing up." She faltered, not sure how to go on.

"I take it you found something out there? Did those Grayson boys mess it up, honey? We told them time and time again not to go hunting out there — nothin' but squirrels, anyway."

"No, sir, it wasn't that." Helen sighed with relief as Beth took over, her soft voice tempered with official coolness. "We found something that shouldn't have been there."

"What was it? Go on and tell me, I won't keel out on you yet." Helen fixed her eyes on her grandfather's face as Beth related the events of the afternoon. He remained calm and still, his breath coming and going in a steady rasping sound. Beth finished quickly, telling only the salient details. Silence filled the room until the old man spoke.

"You want to know about the house, don't you? That's why you've come here." He raised a thin trembling hand to his forehead, as if memory lay beneath the gnarled fingers. "We laid that foundation in 'fifty-eight? No, 'fifty-nine, it was. Summertime. I remember 'cause of how hot it was."

"Can you tell me who was working on it, sir?"

"Let me see. Guess those Johnson boys worked on it — and maybe Jimmy Grayson. I did some of it myself. No, I think those Johnsons did most of it. Good boys — did a good job."

"Tom Johnson? Who had the produce stand out by Corinth?" Helen asked.

Beth and Sheriff McCormick both glanced at her in surprise, as if they'd forgotten she was there. "That's right. I remember some folks talked a bit 'cause of me hiring colored boys for the work when there was plenty of white men needed a job."

"And Tom died last year," Helen said as Beth began making notes on a small pad.

"Yes, he did. His oldest boy is living with Lois out by Corinth now." His eyes followed the movement of Beth's pen across the page, and Helen felt his hand slip from hers.

"Any of Tom's brothers still around?" Beth asked.

"I expect so. Wait — I think Roby, the younger one, is out in Jackson. Headin' some kind of construction crew out where they're building that civic center, just off Highway Twenty."

Beth slipped the pad back into her pocket. "You planned that house yourself, didn't you?"

"Sure did." A grin tugged at his mouth. "Same year this doll-baby was born. Did a lot of the work on it, too." His lips clamped shut. "Ask Maud," he rasped. His voice had been cracking for the last few sentences, and now he gave way to belabored breaths. "Plans somewhere around."

Beth leaned over the bed and looked closely at his drawn face. "Sheriff, I'm so sorry we had to bother you like this. Specially when you haven't seen your granddaughter in so long." Helen watched as Beth quickly located the button that alerted the nurses' station, and in moments they were being shuffled out of the room and down the hall.

Helen leaned against the wall as they waited for the elevator. Beth twirled her sunglasses in her hands, waiting for Helen to enter first. The doors slid silently shut, and with a lurch they started for the ground floor.

"What are your plans, Helen?"

"I haven't even thought about it." Remembering the heat outside, and the rocky ride in Loy's truck, Helen had a sudden desire to simply remain within the four walls of the elevator. "Guess I'll have to go back to Cousin Maud's and meet the relatives."

"Why don't you call them and say you're going to grab a bite with me? I'll drive you back up to Corinth later."

Helen stared. "All the way back to Corinth? Beth, that's close to three hours! I can't ask you to do that!"

"Well, you can always stay overnight at my place." Beth avoided Helen's eyes as she spoke. The doors opened and they were facing the underground garage. "I could take you back in the morning. I have the day off tomorrow."

"Well —" Helen was too tired at that moment to do anything but be led. "Are you sure?"

"We can call them before we leave. Phone's over there."

Wearily Helen dug in her purse for some change as Beth pulled the patrol car beside her. As she waited for Maud to answer, Helen watched Beth staring across the garage. With a strange sense of certainty Helen knew that Beth would ask her about her cousin Bob's presence in Tupelo last night. Anger and disappointment fought inside her as Maud went to fetch Aunt Edna to the phone.

Chapter Seven

Helen didn't recognize the singer wailing on the jukebox. Someone must have brought in a roll of quarters to feed its gleaming hulk. Country music had been moaning across the diner for nearly an hour. From the booth she shared with Beth Helen could see, beyond the plastic-domed mounds of doughnuts and apple pie displayed on the counter, three men playing a noisy game of pool. The pasty-faced fry cook, whose pallid skin looked as though it hadn't seen daylight in years, mumbled to the elderly black man who moved silently and smoothly in the depths of the kitchen.

Beth held out a cigarette. "Smoke?"

Helen grinned as she took a cigarette — her second in two days. "I quit. Thanks anyway." She leaned forward as Beth held the lighter for her. The smoke burned down her throat and Helen felt a sense of well-being. She looked down at the greasy remnants of chicken-fried steak and mashed potatoes left on the thick white plate. "This was a good idea. I didn't think a could eat a bite."

"You looked like you needed a break back in the hospital," Beth said.

Helen relaxed against the vinyl cushions. "I didn't expect to find such a welcome." She tapped the cigarette over the ashtray, glancing up at Beth. How much should she ask? "I wonder," she began, "how long it will take to find out who it is?"

Beth shrugged and swirled the ice in her glass. "We may never know, Helen. I wouldn't want to take bets on how many bodies we might find out in the woods around here. Especially dating from the late fifties."

A chill swept over Helen. "Lynching parties."

"Can't pretend it never happened, Helen. Warren County had its share of disappearances."

Images of the battered body of Emmett Till, fire hoses turned on demonstrators, and the unrestrained hatred of white faces, twisted and contorted with rage before television cameras, surfaced in Helen's mind. "I guess there must be records of missing persons still around," she said.

Beth studied her with cool blue eyes. "I'll have to

do some digging. Don't worry, Helen. I'm certain your grandfather had absolutely no knowledge of any of this. Anybody could have taken advantage of a ready-made grave. And Robert McCormick doesn't have a mean bone in his body."

Helen felt irritated with the way Beth was able to read her mind. It had made her mad when they were kids, and she didn't like it any better now. To screen her anger, Helen surveyed the room. The black assistant had emerged from the kitchen and was mopping up tables, working his way slowly around the long narrow room. He paused by their booth and nodded to Beth.

"Evenin'," he said in a soft voice.

"Hey, Joe Nathan, how you doin'?"

"Gettin' along. Heard you was kind of busy this afternoon, out by that house on Pemberton Road, where Ruth McCormick used to live." He swiped at the booth behind him and looked curiously at Helen.

"I'm afraid so. Joe, do you remember Helen Black?"

Recognition spread over his lined face, and Helen had a dim memory of the local jack-of-all-trades who used to help out the McCormick family with a variety of tasks. She was saddened to see how the years had treated him. The big strong hands were curled with arthritis, and the limp that had only been a hint before now halted his walk with evident pain. He took the hand she held out to him.

"I was awful sorry to hear about your aunt," he said in a melodic voice. "She was a good woman."

"Thank you. I'm surprised you remember me," Helen said. "I was just a little brat running around, getting in your way."

His response was interrupted by shouts from the pool room. "Hey, Joe! We need a few more beers in here!" One of the men emerged from the room, cue in hand, the stench of his sweat mingling with the odors of greasy meat and fried potatoes. When he caught sight of Beth and Helen he leaned against the doorway and whistled. "Will you get a look at that! Why, honey, you don't have to get dressed up for me!" He made his way across the diner, revealing the state of his sobriety by stumbling across a chair. Without ceremony he plopped onto the seat next to Beth. Her withering stare would have shriveled anyone less inebriated.

"This is your, uh, 'friend'?" He leered at Helen. His buddies had gathered by the entrance of the pool room, and Helen could hear them sniggering beneath the twang of a steel guitar on the jukebox. "Don't believe we've met." His eyes roved over her with bleared interest.

"You remember Don Watson, don't you, Helen?" Beth stared down at the table and shrank away from the man who leaned heavily against her.

Helen froze as the memory came back — Beth and Don caught necking behind the high school, going as homecoming king and queen to the senior prom, wearing each others' class rings. Helen's own inner struggles with her feelings about Beth in those days had left painful scars that burned to the touch.

"Helen? Not Helen Black?" Don drew himself up in surprise, his staring grating on her again. "You've lost a few pounds, girl. I wouldn't have recognized you."

"You always were a sweet-talker, Don. A real ladies' man." Helen felt her anger dissolving into distaste. What could he do to her now? She glanced over at Joe Nathan, who'd scuttled off to the kitchen in search of beer, an odd expression stealing over his aging face.

"Yeah. Too bad they ain't any ladies in this room."

Beth shoved him away from her and picked up the check. "We have to get going now, Don. You boys stay out of trouble." He backed away, sweeping his flabby bulk down in a mock bow as the two women headed for the cashier.

"Trouble? Me? Why, perish the fucking thought." Encouraged by guffaws from the back room, Don pursued them, mincing his steps behind them. "Please don't hurt me, Officer Dyke! Don't stick me in the ground all carved up! I promise to be a good boy!"

Beth's back stiffened, and suddenly the laughter died. The fry-cook took their money hurriedly, his pale face nervous as he avoided looking at anyone. Beth held her hand out for the change. "I think the boys are waiting to finish their game, Don." She strode out quickly, nearly knocking Helen over as they went out the door into the heavy air of the August night.

"What the hell was that all about?" Helen ventured as the patrol car rolled across the dark streets.

Beth fidgeted while they waited for a light to turn green. Finally she spoke, her voice flat and empty. "Not much. Believe it or not, that asshole is heading up some kind of citizens' action committee that supposedly is going to apprehend our mass murderer. Besides being a good excuse to get drunk, those boys have fun shouting and hollering about how the police aren't doing their job. That kind of shit."

Helen looked out the window. "Not to mention a lot of water under the bridge between you and Don. I always thought you were going to get married."

Beth's laughter rang brightly through the air. "My God, Helen! Even I'm not that stupid! He's been through two wives already, and about five times that many jobs."

Helen decided to ignore the pleasure Beth's laughter gave her. She settled back into the seat, sleepy and full of food. "It's too bad you have to put up with that kind of crap."

Beth shrugged. "Goes with the territory, Helen. This isn't Berkeley, in case you hadn't noticed. It's not always easy being the town queer."

Helen glanced at her. "That bad?"

Beth snorted. "You should know. You took off out of here like a bat out of hell quite a number of years ago."

"I didn't have much choice, Beth."

They drove on in silence for a while. To break the tension Helen asked about the recent series of murders.

Beth grimly stared out at the dark road ahead. "I guess it won't make much difference if you have a few facts to spread around back in California. What do you know now?"

"Just what the papers said. All young black women."

"Right. All of them raped, mutilated, strangled. Hands tied behind their backs. We haven't found anything like hairs or fabric or skin from the killers yet —"

"More than one person?"

"Well, it seems to be pretty much a gang-bang session. The only common factors with these girls are that they're black, and that they're very young. The oldest was fifteen. I'll tell you something, Helen. I've seen some ugly sights in my day. Hunting accidents, stabbings, lots of beating and bruising, car wrecks. But this is bad. Really bad. Someone out there is full of hate."

Beth's words were cold and hard in the dark. The memory of the bones beneath Aunt Ruth's house emerged, unbidden, in Helen's mind. "Maybe some kind of racist organization? Skinheads, neo-Nazi groups? Although the KKK is trying hard these days to be socially acceptable."

"That's the first place we looked, of course. Especially with that shithead in Louisiana who ran for office. But people like that like to leave some kind of signature behind. A swastika, or the good old stars and bars, something like that. These guys leave nothing behind that we've found yet. Just some poor child all cut up, her clothes ripped apart, tossed out in the dirt."

"Tire tracks?"

"Different every time. There's either a bunch of people in on this, or they have access to a lot of different vehicles. Pickups, vans, all types of four-wheel drives. You want to take bets on how many of those are in Warren County?"

"Someone who works with cars, then. A mechanic, an auto dealer —"

Beth nodded. "We're working on that." Helen was

warned off pursuing the topic in more detail by the defensive edge that crept into Beth's voice. She went on. "What's really worrying us now, also, is the fact that this last one was found up in Tupelo. These shitkickers doing all this are expanding operations."

"I wonder —" Helen hesitated. She looked out over the dimly lit streets of Vicksburg. The headlights from passing cars, few and far between, flashed across her line of vision, illuminating the houses that rested on crooked foundations. Helen recognized this part of town. Beth apparently lived in the poorer section, still faintly respectable but crumbling a bit around the edges.

"What do you wonder?"

"The body at Aunt Ruth's. Maybe it's a young black girl, a teenager, raped and mutilated and strangled."

"A good possibility. Forensic should have some information for us in a couple of days. We'll probably send some of the remains over to Jackson. They have better facilities than we do out here." Beth was steering the car into a driveway as she spoke. Helen caught a glimpse of a small, neat white clapboard house, with a carefully tended lawn and potted plants on the front porch.

Helen felt a strange mixture of emotions as they walked up the steps. She hadn't been alone with this woman in over fifteen years, and the last time they'd laid eyes on each other it was while making love in the backseat of Helen's car. Helen's mood was shattered when Beth said abruptly, "There are a few things I need to talk to you about, Helen."

The screen door squeaked open, protesting mildly as Helen held it while Beth turned the key in the lock. "What things?" she asked, although she was sure she knew the answer.

They walked inside. "Mostly about your cousin Bob. And his late-night excursions to Tupelo."

Chapter Eight

Don Watson stumbled back into the pool room where the others waited, watching him expectantly. The stench of too many beer bottles filled Don's nostrils, mingling with the lingering tang of unwashed male bodies crowded into a dingy room with poor ventilation. One man chalked a cue, his eyes avoiding Don's, grimy hands twisting the thin length of wood around and around. Another man sucked a bottle dry, then tossed it in the corner with a belch. A third crouched in another corner, his bald pate shiny with sweat under the glare of the light that swung overhead.

"So —" The bald man got up, drew himself up to his full height of well under six feet, and scratched his lean belly. "What are we gonna do about them sons of bitches in the police department?"

Don snorted and grabbed a cue. As he leaned over the pocked and uneven table a grin crawled over his broad oily face. "We ain't got nothin' to worry about from them fuckers. Besides, they'd all be on our side, anyway."

"Except for that dyke. She hates your fat guts," snickered Don's opponent. His humor was rewarded with a brief but effective slap that nearly toppled him to the ground. "Shit, Don, I was only kidding around." He scrambled to regain his balance and looked to the others for confirmation.

"I don't want to hear her name ever coming out of that shithole you call a mouth." He propped his cue against the table and glanced over his shoulder into the deserted diner. Joe Nathan was nowhere to be seen, and the cook was busily making noise in the kitchen. "Anyhow, we got work to do."

The others grouped around him, their eyes suddenly hard and glittering. The beer bottles stood forgotten, lined against the wall. "Where this time, Don?"

Don surveyed his minions, savoring the moment of power. "John's got a repair job lined up over in Meridian. Plenty coon hunting out there, wouldn't you say?"

* * * * *

Robert McCormick had given up trying to figure out what time it was. Since he had to be fed intravenously, even mealtimes were a thing of the past. The same gray light always seemed to shine both inside and outside the hospital, day and night. Sleep was an intermittent relief, which he was only able to obtain with drugs. When was it that Beth and Helen had stood beside him in this room? Yesterday? Ten minutes ago? He blinked, listening to the quiet hum and pulse of the machinery that gave him a tenuous hold on life. Although he felt the heavy fog drifting over his thoughts, he knew there was something he had to think about. Something he had to tell someone about. Was it Helen? Seeing her had stirred up so many things that lay frozen for years in his memory. He seemed to see Helen at various ages parading before him — a pudgy adolescent, shy and awkward, a sturdy tomboy in jeans and T-shirt, and now the slender dark woman with the unreadable face staring down at him with pity in her eyes.

He looked at the photographs framed on the table near the bed. It didn't matter that the details were indecipherable to him. Both pictures were grooved into his mind like deep cuts into clay. The face of his dead wife, recorded in black and white, was now more real to him than her living features had ever been. And the lurid picture of the police squadron, in the candy-colored tints of the early sixties, burned across his mind as if the men were standing in the room. A tear slowly cut a path across his cheeks drawn taut with pain. Yes. Helen. He had to tell her. Had to tell her something.

* * * * *

Loy and Edna made the turnoff onto the gravel road in total darkness that was broken only by one headlight from the pickup — the other had gone out as they left Vicksburg. Loy glanced over at his wife leaning against the passenger door, her hand covering her eyes. Another headache, he knew. He edged carefully across the rocks, hoping she was asleep and that the movement of the truck wouldn't wake her.

"Do you think Helen's all right, staying with Beth?"

"Sure, honey. Don't worry about it." He patted her arm gently. "Probably do her good to get away from family for a little bit."

"Beth knows something." Edna removed her hand and stared up into the dark sky. "She wasn't just being polite, showing up at Maud's like that."

"Now, honey, we don't know —"

"Loy, I'm tellin' you, she wants to find out about Bobby. Do you think — do you think Helen will say anything?" She turned to him, her face tense with worry.

Loy sighed. For the past three hours of their drive to Corinth he'd been trying not to think about that. "Darlin', there isn't anything to tell. Helen's smart. She was a cop herself once, you know." The thought wasn't comforting, so Loy swiftly changed the subject. "Maud was looking pretty good, wasn't she? We ought to get down there more often."

The familiar facade of their home loomed up before them. They clambered out of the truck and Loy helped his wife up the porch steps. All the lights were ablaze, but Bob was nowhere to be found.

"All the guns are here, thank God." Relieved, Loy examined the gun rack mounted on the paneling. "He must be around here somewhere."

Edna had already walked through the kitchen and was now peering out through the screen door that led to the small backyard. "He's out here, Loy. Son, what's wrong?"

Loy followed her out, his stomach shriveling. He stood on the back steps, holding the screen door open, watching his family. Edna had frozen on the thin grass. A hand flew to her mouth in horror, and she turned a white face pierced by shocked, glittering eyes back to Loy. Cold resignation settled on his shoulders as he joined her.

Their son was perched like an oversized child on the ancient swing-set. The rusted metal swing groaned under his hunched weight. Tears made shiny tracks through the grime caked on his face, and he moaned in an unceasing, low undertone. Bob's hands were fisted in his coat pockets, and he visibly trembled before them.

Edna failed to conceal the fear in her voice as she leaned over her son. "Bobby, baby, what's the matter? Won't you tell Mama what's wrong?"

Loy gasped as Bob withdrew his hands from his pockets. He held out his arms to his parents, and Edna reached her short plump arms around him, smearing herself with clay and mud in the embrace. "It's all right, sweetheart, don't cry. Mama's here." Loy patted Bob on the shoulder as he stared at his son's hands. The blood was not quite dried yet, and it smeared from Bob's palms onto the back of Edna's dress, leaving vague, messy prints on his mother's back as if she'd been wounded.

* * * * *

Beth lay on the fold-out sofa bed in her living room and tried not to listen to Helen's breathing. She shut her eyes, rolled over, and told herself for the hundredth time that dawn would soon arrive and she had to get a few hours' sleep. Helen stirred, sighed in her sleep, and Beth felt a rush of desire flood her body. Christ, wouldn't she ever get over this? It was so many years ago. They'd both changed so much. Beth reviewed the evening in her mind. Had she revealed any of her feelings to Helen? There had been moments — hearing Helen's laugh, watching the way she'd turned her face to hide her expression, the exhaustion in her eyes. Beth had almost reached out to touch her several times but fear had held her back. Helen had every right to be angry at Beth for the past.

With a sigh of exasperation Beth tossed back the sheets and padded softly to the kitchen. She was standing right next to the wall telephone when it rang. Beth grabbed it on the first peal, hoping it hadn't roused Helen.

"Yes?" she said in a low voice.

"That you, Beth?"

"What's up, Charlie?" She looked out of her kitchen window at the faint pink streaks in the sky. A bird flew across the horizon, a tiny black dot cutting through the first gray light of the day. She felt her stomach knot as she heard Charlie's familiar monotone, already knowing what he was going to tell her. A movement behind her told her that Helen was up. She turned to see Helen's pale face beneath the tousled dark hair.

"Got another one, Beth. Up in Yazoo City this time."

"Fuck," Beth breathed. She leaned against the wall. Helen, her eyes instantly alert, moved closer. Beth avoided her gaze, listening. "Okay, Charlie. Yeah, I know. Okay. I'll be there in a bit." She hung up.

"Where?" Helen asked in a toneless voice. Beth told her, watching her expression. It was blank. "That's right above Vicksburg, isn't it?"

"Yeah." Beth yawned and opened the refrigerator door in search of food. "Bill Campbell from Yazoo called us down here. Wanted to know if we were interested. Interested! Shit, the man has got to be a rocket scientist."

Helen scratched her head. "I guess I can rent a car to get back to Corinth."

"If you don't mind hanging around with me for a while I could run you back later." Beth reached for the milk.

"Sure," Helen said in a practiced nonchalant tone.

"Besides, it will give me a chance to talk to Bobby." She shut the refrigerator door and glanced at Helen, who turned away, clearly angry and upset, clearly unwilling to face Beth any longer.

In spite of the August heat, it was cold inside the trailer. The man hunched over the newspaper sipped at scalding black coffee as his eyes searched the columns of newsprint. At last he found what he was looking for, and the painful intensity of his bony frame relaxed slightly. The obituary of Ruth McCormick took up quite a bit of space. He scanned the names of the relatives who attended the funeral, chuckling now and then as he envisaged how each one would react to the reading of the will. Of course, his name — John William Black — wasn't there, and never would be associated with any of those damned McCormicks again. Ever since his wife died and his one and only child had turned out to be a pervert —

He cut short his thoughts, knowing that he'd only aggravate that ulcer if he let himself go on. The McCormicks were all damned, anyway. Let the unbelievers rot in hell. He read his daughter's name and felt an odd twinge. How many years since he'd seen her? An ache that had nothing to do with the ulcer stole over him, and he could still feel his upraised arm coming down on her head with a sickening slap.

He drained the cup and started pacing, up and down, across the narrow floor of the trailer. Outside the Big Black River gurgled thickly in the morning air that was already promising another scorcher. Helen would know by now that Ruth's old house belonged to her. Would she have gone out there yet? Even if she had, John was willing to bet she wouldn't have found a thing. Besides, she'd just as soon get rid of the place and get back to California. Back to her sin and depravity.

John stood still. At his feet, Susie, his aging hound, whined. "Hang on, I'll feed you in a minute." An idea began to form in his head. He remained standing, letting it take shape. Yes, yes. It might just work. But he'd need the day off. He figured the hardware shop could get along without him for a day or so. As the sun edged over the hills and lit the dark sheen of the river, John sat down with a fresh cup of coffee and worked out his plan.

The household was just beginning to stir when Frieda returned from her morning run. Janice and Claire, the two women who were putting her up for the week, murmured to each other from the sanctity of the bedroom. Frieda started the coffee and found the English muffins. Their warm, yeasty scent filled the kitchen. As soon as she'd had a bite to eat, she had to hit the showers. It was going to be a very busy day — meetings with a couple of gallery owners, lunch with the UCLA professor who hoped to coax her to stay for a semester, the talk that evening at the women's center.

While munching on a muffin Frieda picked up the newspaper. Idly she scanned the headlines until her eyes rested on the word MISSISSIPPI near the bottom of the front page. The muffin lay forgotten on a saucer as she read the story, then headed for the telephone.

Chapter Nine

Helen yawned, stretched, felt the unfamiliar rustle of Beth's clothes against her skin. The jeans and shirt fit loosely — Beth had gained a few pounds over the years — but the fabric felt soft, somehow comforting. Helen had been reluctant but Beth had insisted. "You can't go around in a suit and heels. These should fit you pretty well," and she'd handed the clothes to her with an enigmatic smile on her usually impassive face.

Helen had felt a rush of pleasure she didn't want

to examine or even think about. The idea of spending more time with Beth had been intoxicating.

Hunger was beginning to gnaw at Helen. Restlessly she turned in her chair and looked out the window. The sheriff's office was situated just outside Vicksburg, off the frontage road that ran parallel to Highway 20. The military park lay east of the building. She could make out the tops of some of the monuments — Union, probably, since this location was inside what had been the old Federal siege lines. The cemetery, with its rows of white markers ranged like broken teeth on the dark green grass, was not visible on the ridge that overlooked the river, but Helen saw it clearly in her mind. The hum of the air conditioner brought her back to the present, and she studied the room with interest.

To an outsider, the dilapidated chairs and scarred, scratched desks would give an air of inadequacy to the official activities that took place here. The linoleum, a dull institutional green, bore the grime of years, and the Mr. Coffee on the metal rollaway cart in the corner had seen better, cleaner days. A fly-specked poster about drunk driving hung askew on the wall she faced, as she sat waiting for Beth.

Behind her the battered file cabinets ranged like soldiers. On the other side of a shoulder-high partition to her right was a compact computer setup, where a stocky apple-cheeked youngster was feeding information into the machine. On their way in, Beth had led her past a long, narrow room where Helen had had a glimpse of two officers putting together a scene-of-crime kit that contained all the essentials. They'd greeted Beth and examined Helen closely.

Except for the kid at the computer, Helen was alone. A box of doughnuts, slick with grease, beckoned from the metal cart. Helen gave in to her groaning stomach and walked over to help herself to a doughnut, sneaking a look at the glassed-in office where Beth and the sheriff stood listening to Loy and Edna. Bobby sat in a chair, his back to Helen, rocking back and forth.

The dismal group had met Beth and Helen an hour before on the steps of the station. One glance told Helen that none of them had slept a wink last night. Loy had cleared his throat and scratched his ear as he said that they had something to tell Beth.

"Come on in." Beth ushered them inside with a glance at Helen. Helen felt an uneasy mixture of shame and relief. It had been so hard, the night before, to avoid talking to Beth, telling her openly all that her aunt and uncle had revealed the day before. Beth hadn't pressed the issue, but Helen was sure she would have relented if they'd spent enough time together. Mingled with her other emotions was a sense of sadness at the realization that Beth had only wanted information from her.

At first Helen expected to be included in the gathering in the sheriff's office, but Beth politely pointed her to a chair. After briefly rummaging through a stack of manila folders, Beth had led the others down the hall, asking Helen to wait. "Won't be long," she'd said over her shoulder.

Helen returned to her chair, munching thoughtfully on the doughnut. As she looked around for a napkin to wipe her hands, her eyes roved over the desk and lit on the folders that rested there. She watched the kid bent over the terminal. He was painstakingly entering information, typing with two fingers. Helen took a couple of tissues from the box on the desk and slid the top file onto her lap.

The phone rang with a sharp peal that nearly made her drop the folder. When the kid answered his face lit up, and he murmured into the receiver. A girlfriend. Good. Keeping one ear intent on the office down the hall, Helen opened the file.

This was the right one. Photographs of Aunt Ruth's house were stacked on top of the reports. At the bottom of the pile were pictures of the pitiful remains they'd dug up yesterday afternoon. Helen skimmed the coroner's notes — female, black, probably about fifteen, buried there for at least thirty years. More information would be coming in the next few days, Helen guessed, once tests had been run in Jackson. Somehow the girl's dress had been partially preserved in the thick red clay. Helen felt a wave of sadness as she studied the remnants of what must have been a party dress. The photographer had done his job well. Her eye was caught by a missing strip of gold and white cloth, neatly cut away rather than torn or ripped. The sight of the clean edges bothered her.

There was nothing recorded in the file to indicate cause of death — that was a job for the techs in the lab — but the position of the body indicated that the girl had been either dead or unconscious when buried. The final pages of the report described a search of the house and grounds, but after nearly four decades there was little left to find. A computer printout stuck in the back showed a request for a records search on all missing young black females since 1950. Helen shook her head, knowing from experience how tedious and fruitless such a search was apt to be. Dental records, of course, were always a possibility, but given the time and place, it was quite likely that the girl hadn't ever visited a dentist. Helen thought of her grandfather, lying in pain and drug-induced stupor in the hospital. They'd have to go back and try to get more information from him.

The plural pronoun stayed in her mind as Helen pictured Beth, standing at her side, strong and comforting, in the hospital. Shoving that image aside, Helen went back to the file after a quick look assured her that Don Juan at the computer was still on the phone.

The sickening facts etched on the page gripped her insides. Many of the bones were broken in several places, and one hand had been almost completely severed. The spine had snapped near the neck. That might not have been the cause of death, but the severe mangling must have been excruciating for the victim. Helen hoped the damage had occurred after the girl was lifeless. What sort of bestial bacchanal had taken place on the poor thing?

She sorted quickly through the rest of it. A thin gold chain was found beneath the body — not hung around the neck, but placed in the earth under the remains. Helen stared at it, noting its dull gleam against the red soil, the sheen not completely crusted over with dirt. She checked the notes again — yes, real gold, the Vicksburg lab had stated. Was a black girl from the bottomlands of the Delta likely to have such a costly item? And why was it laid like this beneath her, and not draped from her neck when she dressed? The chain itself was unbroken, so it hadn't been torn from her. A few shreds of plastic and a metal clasp eaten away by time and decay were all that remained of a handbag. No evidence of shoes.

Helen looked up as the kid replaced the receiver with a satisfied smirk on his face. He poked at the computer with increased vigor, but his expression revealed that his thoughts were far away. Still no sound from the end of the hall. Helen went back to the photographs of the corpse. There was something wrong about all this — something that didn't fit. What the hell was it?

She forced her mind to relax, to sink into total concentration on the pictures. No thoughts, no analysis, just complete blankness, allowing the details of the horrible portrait to soak in, as if it were simply a problem in aesthetics. The deep cavity in the earth, the clods of clay that clung to the remains, the thin white length of bone that lay shrouded in tatters.

As the phone shrilled again Helen sat back in her chair, the file lying loosely in her lap. She watched the kid's eyes roll up in disgust.

"Yes, Miz Shelby. Arabs this time? Yesterday when you called it was two Japanese men that broke into your house, remember?" He looked over at Helen, shaking his head and inviting her to share his amusement. "Well, did they hurt you any? Or take anything? Uh huh."

Helen smiled at him absently. She had it, finally. It wasn't any one detail about the body. It was the whole scene. Why would anyone inflict this kind of mutilation on a young woman, then lay her out carefully in a grave? Surely if her killer — or killers — had abused her as if she were a senseless doll, they would have tossed her into the ground without ceremony, without any concern for appearances. They would want only to ensure that no trace of themselves would be found. She'd assumed from the beginning that this had been the work of young studs out to prove their manhood during a time when the black community was very easy prey. No questions asked, no punishment meted out for terrorism.

Unless — and this was worse — unless the murderers had some sort of fixed ritual surrounding the burial. Perhaps this arrangement of the body gratified some awful need for ceremony. She looked again at the alignment of shattered bones, the precise positioning of the severed hand back to the arm. And the necklace — what sort of totem did that represent?

Helen closed the file and looked at the other folders stacked on the desk. She ached to look through them, to see if they contained photos of the victims found recently. Had they, too, been neatly arrayed for interment, or tossed in a heap beneath a thin layer of dirt?

She slid the file back on top of the others as the door to the sheriff's office opened. Later she'd try to make a few notes for herself, while it was all still fresh on her mind. Standing up, Helen walked toward the hall. Edna and Loy scurried out, faces down, too embarrassed and miserable to face her. Bob stumbled between them, his expression oddly peaceful. He looked around him with interest, smiled at Helen, then disappeared into the heat and light of the day as his parents guided him to the entrance.

Beth sighed and rubbed her face as she stood by

her desk, looking down at Helen. "Come on. We're going for a ride."

Helen suddenly felt excited and happy. She didn't know if it was from the mental exercise or from the thought of accompanying Beth. "Only if you promise to find us some food. I've had one doughnut this morning, and my stomach is complaining."

"We'll get something on the way to Yazoo City."

Helen climbed into the car and Beth pulled away from the station and headed for the highway. Vicksburg receded into the background as Helen said, "The scene of the crime. I feel honored to be tagging along."

Beth smiled and slid her sunglasses over her eyes. "You have to promise to be a good girl, though."

"Absolutely." Helen smiled out the window as they sped north.

Chapter Ten

Beth turned off the main highway and headed west. Helen stuffed the remains of their fast-food breakfast into a paper sack that was heavily spotted with grease. She shielded her eyes from the glare of the sun and wished she'd brought sunglasses.

"That's all Bobby said?"

"Yep." Beth slowed the car as they approached an intersection. "Just babbled about water and somebody being hurt."

"When will you get the results back from the lab on the bloodstains?"

"Later today. It's getting priority at Jackson." They had gone south at the intersection, and Helen saw the outskirts of Yazoo City to her left as a backdrop to Beth's profile. "He still doesn't seem to know what happened to your uncle's hunting knife." Beth sighed and rested an arm on the window. "I sure wish you'd told me some of this last night."

"Come on, Beth, what do you want? This is my family. You know as well as I do that Bobby would never hurt anyone, ever." Even as she spoke, Helen felt doubt creeping into her thoughts. What did she know anymore about Bobby? What kind of violence might be suppressed in his brawny, overgrown body and his befuddled mind?

"Of course he didn't! But I think it might have been easier to talk to him in his own home, without a lot of policemen staring at him. And it might have saved your aunt and uncle some grief, too."

"Oh, I get it. You're just thinking of me and my relatives," Helen responded. "Well, isn't that nice to know that you have a heart of gold beneath that badge. It certainly would have been more pleasant for you to weasel out some information over milk and cookies with Loy and Edna."

"Come off it, Helen."

But Helen barged ahead, torn between hurt and anger. "I suppose that's what dinner and staying at your place was all about. Just to see if you could cast some kind of spell over me, get me all starry-eyed and nostalgic, then rip me open."

As soon as the words shot out of her mouth Helen knew they were a big mistake. Beth stared ahead, her face pale and stony, her hands rigid on the steering wheel. Helen, her cheeks burning with shame, slouched against the door. It was too late. The snarling remarks couldn't be taken back now. Except for the indecipherable rumblings of the radio the rest of the short drive out to the Big Black was completely silent.

The thin silvery band of water gleamed up from the narrow bed where it ran northeast, a meager trickle in comparison to its sister a few miles west. The quiet countryside, heavy with lush green foliage and redolent with heat, was broken by the intrusion of police vehicles. An ambulance rested unevenly on the steeply sloping bank, and a cluster of brown-shirted officers were grouped behind the yellow tape stretched in a square at the top of the slope. The roots of an enormous and ancient tree bulged through the mud that had been churned up to conceal the grisly discovery. Long gray strands of Spanish moss, like loose ghostly threads, drifted across the shoulders of the police photographer crouched over the gap in the dirt. A faint cool breeze moved across the river, stirring the leaves overhead, and Helen watched as a large black bird — probably a crow, too small for a hawk — cried out with raucous intensity and flew across the water into the hot blue sky.

Helen stayed in the background, leaning against the patrol car, as Beth approached her colleagues near the tree. They all seemed to know each other. One man led Beth across the patch of ground to view the body. Helen's embarrassment faded with the growing desire to look at the crime scene. Had it been laid out carefully for burial, or tossed in a pathetic heap? From what she could see at a distance, there hadn't been much of a grave — just a shallow hole scooped out. She moved to the other side of the car, hoping to get a better look, so intent on the group beneath the tree that she didn't hear the van pulling up behind her until it had slithered to a screeching halt just a few feet away.

Before the engine was turned off, the huge woman had scrambled out and was running past Helen. She slipped on the wet grass as she ran but managed to keep her footing. Her black skin gleamed with sweat and her eyes glittered with fear. The driver of the van, a grizzled old man with yellowed eyes, hobbled after her, his expression numb and blank. A cold nausea swept over Helen. These people had to be related to the dead girl.

The police looked on with mingled expressions of pity and sternness. Two of them, a man and a woman, were gently restraining the grief-stricken couple from coming any closer. Everyone here knew one another, Helen reminded herself. What were the convoluted relationships they'd all had with one another, unspoken connections that either bypassed or formed bonds across generations of segregation?

"Let me see my baby! I got to see her, I got to know if it's true!" Her screams carried, echoing against the trees. More birds, disturbed from their seclusion, stirred and flew off in a chorus of protest. Her elderly companion stood mute, hands loose at his sides, helpless and still.

Beth looked over at Helen, her face tense with sympathy. Without thinking Helen hurried forward, ducking under the yellow tape. She bent forward to take the woman's arm. "What's her name?" she asked the closest deputy.

"May Hawkins." The deputy looked away to hide

his own emotion. "This here's her youngest. I went to school with her —" He stopped and cleared his throat.

"Mrs. Hawkins?" The woman moaned endlessly, her heavy body swaying back and forth upon her knees, tears streaming down her cheeks. "Mrs. Hawkins, please come back here with me. I promise you, we aren't leaving her here. Please."

Gently Helen persisted, aided by the old man who had come up from behind them. "May, come on. Come on now, let these men do they job."

Helen looked down into the shallow crevice in the earth where the Hawkins girl lay. Unlike the remains in the photographs taken yesterday, this body huddled in a broken heap in the red dirt. The girl's small hands were held up to her battered throat. Helen steeled herself to look closely at the condition of the girl's clothing. Torn underwear had been tossed beside her, while her dress was twisted around her splayed limbs where the killer or killers had shoved it aside. As she helped Mrs. Hawkins back up to her feet, Helen saw clearly that a portion of the hem had been cut away — a narrow strip perhaps eighteen inches long, snaking around the bottom of the dress. Helen mentally stowed these details away as the three of them broke through the tape and headed back to where the van was parked along the river's edge, Mrs. Hawkins stumbling now and then, still moaning.

They reached the police van just as the clouds overhead released a downpour. All morning the sky had been darkening, and thunder had sounded against the bluffs to the west. Helen and her two companions settled into the van. Rain pounded at the windows, covering the sound of Mrs. Hawkins's sobs.

The old man began to speak. "I figured it was all a mistake, but Henry over to the courthouse said we'd better get on out here."

"Henry?" Helen asked.

He turned his yellow, watering eyes to Helen. "He works over there for Judge Heywood. He came to get us and take us to the police station."

"I see." Helen watched as one of the officers — a woman — leaned into the wind, clutching her hat to her head, and pushed her way through the rain to the van. Mr. Hawkins, who was apparently the dead girl's grandfather, rambled on and kept stroking his daughter's arm. Mrs. Hawkins clutched Helen's hand and rocked back and forth against the seat. She seemed not to notice at all as the young officer opened the door and slid onto the passenger seat. Helen tried to release her hand from the distraught woman's grip, but her efforts only made Mrs. Hawkins moan louder.

The officer said, "I'm so sorry, Mrs. Hawkins. I know this is terrible for you — it is for all of us, to see Jenny this way — but I do have to ask you some questions so we can find out what happened."

Helen, at a glance from the young woman, tried once again to ease her way out of the van, but Mrs. Hawkins squeezed her hand in an iron grip, as if it were her only connection to life. Helen knew she wasn't even aware of what she was doing, and the officer sighed and nodded, signaling a reluctant acceptance of the stranger's presence.

The story came out in fragments, pieced together

by the old man as it tumbled from his daughter's lips. Jenny had gone last night to choir practice at the local Baptist church. There was to be a party afterwards. "That's why she had on that dress," her mother gasped. "I told her she looked so pretty."

"She wasn't supposed to walk home." The deputy turned to Mrs. Hawkins's father as he spoke. "I done told her and told her to call us."

She had arranged to spend the night at a girlfriend's house, so her mother and grandfather had not been concerned until the girlfriend called early that morning asking for Jenny.

"Who's the girlfriend?" the officer asked.

"Maggie Jones." He watched while the pen scratched on the notepad. "She didn't know nothin' about this, though."

"Where does she live, Mr. Hawkins?"

"Over by the old school, on French Landing Road. Next to the old Beaudry place, the one they turned into a restaurant."

The sun broke through the clouds, and the rain dwindled to a light pattering against the windows. Helen felt Mrs. Hawkins loosen her grip, and she slowly withdrew her hand. Quietly she opened the door of the van and stepped out, after a glance from the police officer. Fresh cool air, followed by a wave of heat from the emerging sun, bathed her face.

On seeing her Beth walked away from the trees out onto the road. "We won't be long," she said, glancing over her shoulder at the group that remained near the body. "They'll fax me over anything they can by tomorrow."

Helen was about to ask a few questions of her own when a peripheral movement caught her attention. Beth turned back at a call from one of the men, leaving Helen standing alone by the patrol car. Already the sun was glinting with fierce intensity on the water, and Helen shielded her eyes against the light as she gazed across the river.

The battered white Chevy was at least ten years old. It stood directly opposite Helen, across the river, on the frontage road that headed south. The man who got out of the car hobbled with a familiar limp as he edged closer to the river to peer in the direction of the cluster of people around the trees.

Just as Helen recognized who it was, Joe Nathan saw her staring at him, and he lumbered back into his car as fast as his lame leg would allow. With a groan of gears shifted too fast, the Chevy sped off, spitting mud and gravel in its wake.

Chapter Eleven

"What do you suppose Joe Nathan was doing out here," Helen asked as she and Beth walked along the tree-lined banks of the Big Black. The branches overhead shook off drops of water in the breeze.

Beth shrugged. "He's got some folks out here. His brother and sister-in-law, I think. Or maybe he was just curious." She turned her impassive gaze to Helen. "You're not going to suggest he had anything to do with this, are you?"

"No, no. It was just odd, the way he took off like that."

Beth made no comment, and they turned and headed back to where Beth had parked. In the distance Helen saw the brown uniforms of the local police weaving in and out of the patch of ground shaded by the huge tree. Intent on their grisly work, they took no further notice of the two women. Helen, her eyes fixed on the activity, slipped on a clump of wet grass, nearly falling to the ground.

"Careful." Beth's hand suddenly gripped hers as Helen struggled to regain her balance. They stood in shadows, out of sight of the others, a cool breeze spreading over their bodies and carrying the scent of honeysuckle from some distant region. Beth's grasp became a caress. She sighed as her hand traveled up Helen's arm until it reached her shoulder, then her throat, where Beth's fingers gently stroked the vulnerable skin. All the conflicting emotions Helen had been fighting since Beth walked into her cousin's house dissolved into a terrifying tenderness as Helen's hands moved around Beth's waist.

"This is crazy," Helen breathed as Beth pulled her close. "Someone might see us . . ." Her words were lost as Beth kissed her hungrily.

"I don't care, Helen." Beth sighed as she stroked Helen's back. "I've waited too long for this." Slowly she guided Helen farther into the woods, into the darkness and away from the threat of being heard or seen. Her breath was hot on Helen's neck as her hands touched her breasts. Helen gave herself up to the slow lingering kiss, to the strong embrace. "I've dreamed about you for years, all the time you've been in California. Christ, I wanted to see you so much —"

They broke apart abruptly as voices approached.

Helen guessed that the police were spreading out in a search of the area, now that the rain had definitely stopped. She looked over at Beth, who once again wore the smooth, unreadable countenance that had so maddened Helen yesterday.

"This way," Beth said, and Helen followed her through the trees until they came out on the other side of the crime scene. Beth walked over to her colleagues to say a few parting words while Helen went back to the car.

The sun was out hot and intense now, and all around her the moisture from the brief storm melted away in faint wisps of steam. She felt the sweat gathering on her back as they got into the car. Beth backed out, turned, and headed back for the road that would lead them to the highway. They were silent for a few minutes, each aware of the other's presence. Suddenly Beth turned to look at her.

"My uncle's hunting shack is just about a mile west of here," she said. "Remember that place?"

"My God, of course! We used to go out there after school to drink and smoke and be cool!" Helen smiled and shook her head. "It's still standing?"

Beth nodded. "He doesn't go out there to hunt these days, but the cabin's still there. The land's leased out to a timber company now."

Beth took a side road off the highway and Helen began to recognize landmarks. There was the old water tower, now completely rusted out, leaning heavily to one side in the thick undergrowth. The ubiquitous Confederate marker commemorating some long-forgotten skirmish marked the end of the pavement, and the road dwindled to a dirt trail. The patrol car squeezed slowly down the narrow path until they reached a small round clearing sheltered by enormous oaks.

The cabin had stood the test of time fairly well, its weathered walls still firmly rooted in the ground and its roof smooth and even.

"Remember that time we stole a couple of jugs from the Hallandale place? The ones over in Benton?"

"Jesus, I'd forgotten about that." Beth laughed. "It was Halloween, right?"

"Right. That was the first and only time I ever got so bombed. We were both pretty sick." Helen, suddenly light-hearted, opened the cabin door and looked inside. Except for a layer of dust, the interior was tidy. Two ladder-back chairs, leftovers from a thrift shop, stood at a rickety card table in the center of the room. A low bench was placed along the wall opposite the door, beneath a window that allowed a few shafts of light through its accumulation of dirt. At Helen's right was a low, wide cot. The mattress lay bare on the metal frame, and Helen was flooded with memory.

Beth's voice sounded close and warm as she came in behind Helen. "Remember this? This is the first place we ever made love."

Helen fought to control her emotions, not wanting to repeat the scene that had just taken place by the river. "Yes, I remember. It was a long time ago, Beth."

"It feels like yesterday to me."

Helen felt herself leaning back into Beth's embrace, allowing Beth to reach around and caress her breasts. Helen stroked the back of Beth's neck as Beth kissed her shoulders. Without a word Helen turned around and gave in to the hunger, her mouth at first frantic with desire, then slowing into deep, deliberate kisses. Together they sat on the cot, each reaching for the other's clothes.

"This is crazy," Helen whispered as she pushed Beth's shirt off from her shoulders. "We're not a couple of kids anymore."

Beth's response was to lower her mouth to Helen's breast, teasing with her tongue. Helen lay back and closed her eyes as Beth moved downward, stroking her belly. She gasped as Beth's hands gently rubbed between her legs. The cot moved beneath them as their bodies found a rhythm. Beth lay on top of Helen, her hips moving in slow circles, their bodies pressed together. Helen stroked Beth's breasts, heavy and slick with sweat, and watched as Beth's face twisted when she cried out with pleasure.

Beth looked down at her, smiling and panting. "Now it's your turn," and her fingers reached deep inside Helen. Helen heard herself moaning as her body responded to Beth's insistent, gentle pressure. Her senses were flooded and she climaxed quickly, feeling that time had stopped and suddenly they were teenagers again, timidly exploring their bodies and their emotions.

Satiated, Helen closed her eyes. Her body felt drowned in heat as she fell asleep, Beth's head cradled on her neck.

Chapter Twelve

Frustrated, Helen hung up the receiver. Two attempts to reach Frieda had failed. All Aunt Edna could tell her was that her "friend" had called while Helen was out in Yazoo City with Beth. Frieda had left an urgent appeal for Helen to get in touch with her as soon as possible. Helen tried to put anxiety about Frieda out of her mind as she joined the others in the living room. Beth was probably almost back to Vicksburg by now — she'd dropped Helen off two hours ago, wisely choosing not to intrude on Helen's relatives. Helen had been too drained by the events of the past two days to feel much beyond a pleasant lassitude.

The overhead fan in her uncle's home cooled her off a little, and Helen found that she was ravenous once again. Both Edna and Loy were listless, hardly noticing that Helen went into the kitchen and helped herself to some cold fried chicken and a huge slice of pecan pie.

"Where's Bobby?" Helen asked when she returned from the kitchen, her hunger momentarily assuaged.

"In his room. He was asleep a few minutes ago." Edna wiped her forehead, then sat rubbing her fingers as if the motion would rid her of some deep impenetrable pain.

Helen sipped her iced tea, feeling guilty for the sense of well-being that enveloped her while her aunt and uncle were so obviously suffering. "You told the police everything you told me, then?"

Loy nodded. "After we saw him like that, we just couldn't keep to ourselves anymore. He was covered, just covered —" Loy broke off, cleared his throat harshly, then got up from the sofa and began to stomp around the room. When he had regained some control he said, "Better go out and take a look at that motor. I been promising Jack I'd get it back to him," and with a slam of the screen door he disappeared into the afternoon loud with buzzing cicadas.

Edna told the story in bits and pieces, coaxed quietly by Helen. Beth and the sheriff had listened intently, first to their tale of seeing Bobby the previous night, then to Bobby's mumblings. "They just sat there, not taking notes or nothing, looking at all of us as if we was crazy."

"What did Bobby say?" Helen asked, growing impatient with the tears and hand-wringing. Now was no time to hesitate. "If I'm going to be of any help to you, you've got to tell me, Aunt Edna."

Her voice came out small, forced through tight lips. "Just what he told us — that he'd seen a dead body. 'All hurt,' he said. Just like that. 'All hurt. Dead.' "

"Nothing else? Where he'd seen it? Who was with him?"

Edna shook her head. "All he did say was something about water everywhere, and how cold it was." Edna glanced up at Helen, fear and curiosity in her eyes. "You and Beth — did you —"

Helen considered for a moment, then decided it was better to tell her. "We stopped over in Yazoo City on the way here. Another body was found right next to the river."

Edna threw up her hands in a gesture that at any other time, under any other circumstances, would have appeared to Helen as a ridiculous parody of a religious rite. "My Lord, my Lord, what are we gonna do?" she wailed.

Helen rushed to the sofa and forced her hands down. "Calm down, Aunt Edna. It'll be okay. We all know Bobby had nothing to do with this."

"But the sheriff, and Beth!"

"They didn't arrest him, did they? They let him come home with you." Helen spoke with more conviction than she felt. She was certain that an unmarked car was nearby, positioned out of sight but offering a favorable view of the house. All movements, all entrances and exits, would be closely observed.

Helen could feel Edna trembling beneath her reassuring touch. Outside, her uncle, muttering curses and imprecations, was pounding at some mechanical contraption that apparently refused to yield to his will.

"Why don't you lie down for a while, Aunt Edna? You probably haven't had any sleep in a long time."

Loy walked in just as Helen was leading her aunt to the bedroom. He twisted a greasy towel in his blackened hands and looked approvingly at his wife as she lay down.

"I'm goin' out to the pawn shop," he said in an undertone to Helen. "Never did pick up my guns the other day."

They left Edna in the darkened room, and moments later Helen heard the truck groan down the narrow road to the highway.

The house was still. Except for the low buzz of the ceiling fan, the only sounds were insects humming in the yard. Helen, suddenly restless, paced quietly through the house. She passed the master bedroom, where Edna's steady breathing told her that her aunt had drifted into much-needed sleep. Helen hesitated as her steps took her nearer to Bobby's room. The door was ajar, and she listened. Complete silence. Was he sleeping, too? Helen ventured a glance into the room and saw her cousin lying on his cot, his eyes open and staring vacantly at the blank wall. She turned and tiptoed back down the hall to the kitchen.

Helen was surprised to see shadows stealing across the kitchen. It was nearly six-thirty. Where on earth was Uncle Loy? Aunt Edna was still sleeping. The sudden shaft of cool wind that blew across the room warned of another burst of rain on the way, its approach signaled by a low rumbling off to the west. Wondering whether or not she should try to reach Frieda again, she stood by the window lost in thought. She could smell the honeysuckle that Edna had planted along the wall by the kitchen. She had a sudden urge to be outside, to feel the wind moving over her body. To hell with anyone watching the house, she thought as she stepped out the back door.

If she remembered correctly, there was a dirt path that led away from the cluster of trailers and houses into a small patch of woods. Sure enough, here it was. On either side of her the trees, thin and scraggly, arched overhead. Their branches shifted in the wind, and Helen was sharply reminded of the trip up to Yazoo City earlier that day. She stooped down to pick up a stick and continued walking slowly down the path, thinking hard.

She couldn't get over the feeling that there was some kind of connection between the body on Aunt Ruth's property and the girl that had been discovered that morning. The span of more than three decades made it terribly unlikely, of course, that the same person had committed both murders, but the similarities were chilling. It was maddening to know that the facts were neatly sorted and gathered, sitting out of reach in the hands of local authorities, where she'd never get a chance to look at them.

Two bodies, both young women, killed brutally and dumped into the earth. One neatly laid out, as if for burial, the other tossed carelessly with only a token layer of soil over the corpse. And what about the clothing? Was she right about her impression that the most recent victim's dress had been cut into neat strips? Helen kicked angrily at some loose stones on the path, wishing she could come up with a way to go through the records of missing persons in Vicksburg. It was so long ago — maybe all those who would know were all dead and gone.

The image of her grandfather surfaced in her mind. Helen recoiled at the thought of talking to him as he lay dying on the hospital bed, but she knew that was probably the only hope she had of learning anything. He was the only viable link she had to the past. The thought of his death overwhelmed her and she shivered, noticing that the wind had grown sharp and cold. She didn't want to get caught in the rain a second time, so she turned and headed back to the house.

The sound of the wind in the trees almost covered the rustling that followed her. Helen froze on the path, listening hard. The noise contrasted with the movement of the branches, stopping and starting at odd intervals. Slowly Helen made her way back, stopping once again just before the path ended and the expanse of mowed lawn met her at the borders of Loy's property.

There was no mistaking it — someone else was there, walking among the trees. Helen stood still at the edge of the lawn. Clouds covered the sun, and the late-afternoon light disappeared in black shadows. Helen abruptly stepped to her right into the trees — in the direction of the sound. A huge, ancient magnolia, heavy with white blossoms, concealed her as she crouched low, waiting.

She didn't have to hide a long time. There it was again, the sharp crackling of leaves and wood. It was close now, and Helen could detect an odd, uneven quality to the sound, as if the invisible pursuer were hesitating in his or her furtive tracking.

It was now so dark beneath the tree that Helen could just make out the flash of white a few feet in front of her. Through the dense bushes she saw it again, and she held her breath as Joe Nathan passed by. As he emerged onto the path Helen saw that his hands were empty, hanging loosely at his sides. At least she wouldn't have a gun or knife to contend with. He looked around, confused, peering across the lawn to the house. Helen waited for the next noisy gust of wind in the trees before coming up behind him.

Counting on surprise and Joe's lame leg, Helen reached out and twisted his left arm behind his back, jerking just hard enough to cause pain without injury. Her left hand grasped a small sharp stone and she poked it into his back. She prayed he'd be convinced she was holding a gun.

Fortunately her gamble paid off. He didn't even try to struggle. It was as if he'd been expecting a confrontation, even welcoming it.

"What a surprise," Helen breathed. "You should have come right up and knocked on the door, Joe. You didn't have to come sneaking around through the woods."

Joe sighed deeply. "I ain't come to hurt nobody." He briefly tried to turn and face her, but Helen tightened her grip, feeling ashamed of her tactics as she took in his wasted, aging physical condition. "I just — I only wanted —"

"What? What did you want, Joe? And what were you doing out at Yazoo City this morning?"

"I knew you'd seen me. I knew it was up then."

Helen loosened her hold, but he stayed where he was. "That's when I knew I had to tell you."

Helen waited while Joe turned around. His face was invisible in the growing shadows. "Tell me what?"

"The girl at your aunt's house. The dead girl. Mattie."

Chapter Thirteen

Joe Nathan insisted on buying the second round. Helen watched him hobble across the floor to the bar at the end of the shabby room. The vinyl seat of the booth he'd chosen squealed beneath her as she fidgeted, painfully aware of the glances from the solemn black men who sat scattered around the room. Their eyes shifted away whenever she met them, and they continued to drink steadily, quietly, with the devotion of serious drinkers. The jukebox was silent against the wall to her right. Helen turned to watch the rain pelting down on the rusted metal sign that extolled the benefits of drinking Coke. It waved back and forth in the cold wind.

She looked in the direction of the bar to see Joe Nathan making his way toward her, nodding a hello to one of the other patrons. Helen took the bottle from him and drank thirstily.

"I can get you a glass, if you want."

"No, thanks, this is just fine." The shock of cold beer on a parched throat made her eyes water. She blinked hard and managed a grin. "Thanks."

He cleared his throat and wrapped his huge hands around the bottle. "This is the best place I could think of to go and talk. Didn't want to just sit in the car." He took a sip, never taking his eyes off of her. "Hope your folks won't worry about you."

"I left Aunt Edna a note on the fridge." As she leaned across the sticky formica table, Helen's elbow nudged the empty bottle from the first round. "But let's not worry about them right now. You were telling me what happened after Mattie ran away that night."

He closed his eyes tight for a moment, swallowed some more beer, and set the bottle carefully on the table. "It's kind of scrambled up in my head. I was on the ground, but I could see that man who'd grabbed hold of Mattie. He was howlin' — I guess Mattie hit him or somethin' — and he was so mad his face was red. He started to wave his arms around and yell at the others."

"What did he say?"

He shrugged and looked out at the rain. "I was hurtin' pretty bad myself right then. All I could think about was gettin' the hell out of there. My legs hurt so bad I could hardly think." He turned and looked straight at Helen, the memory of pain staring into her own eyes. "One guy kept jumpin' on my legs. Busted my kneecap. Couple of fingers, too. I was only seventeen . . ."

Helen had to look away from those dark, steady eyes. "How did you get away from them?"

"Well, once that guy started yelling — the one who had Mattie — it was like he was leading them somehow. He got all the others gathered around him. Guess they were goin' off to find Mattie. Soon as they let me go I just scooted off around the cars. They must've thought I was out cold, or they was more worried about her gettin' away." His fingers drummed against the table, marking out a staccato rhythm that counterpointed the rain. "I crawled and crawled through the dirt. Seemed like forever. And all the time I was sure they'd come runnin' after me."

"But they didn't."

He shook his head. "Guess Mattie had spooked 'em. By the time I got back to the party, they'd disappeared. Gone off into the woods after her."

"What did you tell the others?"

He snorted, flattening his palms on the table. "Shit, I didn't have to tell them nothin'! They knew it was white boys soon as they got a look at me. You been away a long time — you don't remember what it was like. Still is, too."

"But Mattie — didn't they try to find her?"

"A whole bunch of them went with the preacher out to find her. Looked all night out by the river, but didn't find nothin'. Never did find her. Never."

His voice had faded nearly to a whisper. Helen

leaned forward again, straining to hear, but Joe Nathan had fallen silent. "Why do you think it was Mattie they found under Aunt Ruth's house?"

He licked his lips and sighed. "Because your grandpa came out to see me that night."

Helen fought down the cold panic that surged through her. "He was sheriff then, wasn't he?"

He nodded, his eyes still watching her cautiously. "I don't know what time it was. Someone had taken me home, and I was propped up on the sofa. The doctor — you remember Doc Wilkinson? Only guy in town who would take care of us back then. He'd just bound up my legs and taken off, when in walks Sheriff McCormick." He grimaced at the memory. "I didn't want to have nothin' to do with him. Didn't want to tell him a damned thing. But Mama had called him. She kept sayin' how we could trust him, how he'd always tried to help us." He snorted again, then finished off his beer. "I can still see him, standing over me. He didn't talk, just looked down at me, his eyes goin' to all the different places where I was bandaged. Just standing there, waiting. Waiting for me to start talking."

"What did you tell him?"

"I couldn't help myself. I guess it was the medicine the doctor gave me, on top of being scared shitless. It all just came pouring out of me. All about those bastards, about Mattie disappearing. The whole thing. And him just standing there, his mouth twitching around — you remember how it used to do that? Shit."

Helen broke the silence that followed. "Then what?"

"He left. He listened to me and went away. But

he came back later." He rubbed a hand over his face. It glistened with sweat, and his eyes were turned away from Helen, and from the memory of the pain. "I don't know how much later. They kept me pretty doped up on somethin' — I think it might have been later that night. It was dark, I do remember that much."

"What happened? What did he tell you?"

Joe Nathan snorted. "He didn't tell me a damn thing. Nothing. The man just stood there, lookin' at me again, and watchin' me. I could see his face. He was standin' right there in the doorway, and there was this bulb swingin' overhead. When he opened the door it moved back and forth, back and forth. You could see his face, then it all went dark. Then you saw it again." He shut his eyes, screwed them tight against the remembered image. "He'd seen somethin' awful. His face was all white, and his eyes were so big under that hat. All his clothes was messed up, like he'd been rollin' around in the mud. And he was sweatin', too. Dripping off his face, onto the floor."

"And he didn't say a word." Helen watched him closely. Anything was possible, but she simply couldn't believe he was lying. Even after all these years the fear of that night still gripped him. There was no bitterness or anger in his tale — only terror.

Joe stared at her again. "I tried to talk myself, to ask him what he'd found out there — if Mattie was all right. But when I saw his face I just couldn't talk. It wasn't easy to talk then, anyway. I think I drifted off for a bit, 'cause the next thing I knew he was in the living room, talking to my mother. I could hear his voice — he'd left the door open — but I couldn't make out what he was sayin' to her."

Helen sighed. Her neck ached from the tension she'd built up in it by leaning forward to hear him. As she glanced up she noticed that the bar had emptied. It was night, and a faint rumble in the distance was a reminder of the storm that had just passed.

"That must have been when he gave her the money." Helen's attention snapped back to the man sitting before her. "Musta been quite a bit, too, to take care of me for a few months."

"What do you mean?"

Joe looked at his empty beer bottle. "Want another one? No? Well, after a coupla days my mother sent me away. I went to New Orleans, had a place at a boardin' house there for about six months. I was worried, not knowin' how she could pay for it, but she told me the sheriff was takin' care of all of it, that he'd be sure I was okay."

Keeping him away so he wouldn't talk? Or to protect him? "What did you do there?"

He shrugged. "Nothin', for a while. Just got rested, got my legs back in some kinda shape. After a coupla months I got me a job at a juke joint. Lots of 'em down there, and nobody really cares where you from."

"And what about Mattie?"

His eyes darkened at the mention of the girl's name. His features stiffened and he stared down at his hands as he answered. "I never heard no more about her. I tried to find out from Mama, tried to get her to ask the sheriff about her, but she got real mad at me. Said to keep my nose out of it if I was smart. Once she came down to New Orleans and we got into a big fight over it. I said I was goin' right back to Vicksburg and ask him straight out where she was. Mama just blew up — rantin' and screamin', like she was going to kill me herself. After that I knew."

Helen was puzzled. "Knew what, Joe?"

He finally looked up at her. "That Mama wasn't mad. She was scared. Scared to death."

His gaze wandered out to the parking lot where his Chevy sat in the still, hot air. An eighteen-wheeler rumbled by, chugging its cargo down the lonely two-lane blacktop. Joe stared after it as it disappeared on its way south to Jackson.

"I guess she knew all along that Mattie was dead. There was nothin' she could do about Mattie, but she could still save me."

"By cooperating with the sheriff. With my grandfather." The words tasted bitter as she spoke.

Joe looked at her with pity. "It's nothin' to do with you, you know. You was only a baby when it happened."

Helen fidgeted under his steady gaze, fearful of his sympathy. "When did you come back to Mississippi?"

"It was six, seven months later. My uncle Harold had a fish market down by Hattiesburg — raisin' catfish in a tank, that kinda stuff. I started workin' for him. Never did finish school. Or get this leg fixed, neither."

"And you never found out what happened to Mattie." It came out as a statement rather than a question.

"Oh, I tried — no one wanted to know. Lotsa

folks figured she'd just run off. But I knew she had to be dead. Those bastards weren't gonna let her get away and spoil their fun."

Helen toyed with her napkin. "Did you think my grandfather killed her?"

Joe looked out the window again. "No."

Helen watched him carefully as they got up to leave. Did he really feel that way? The smooth facade had shrouded his face again, and they drove wordlessly back to her uncle's house.

Joe dropped her off at the turnoff that led to the group of converted trailers. Helen, weary in every bone, walked through the heat toward Aunt Edna's, trying to assimilate all she'd learned that day. She could hear arguing before she reached the house — Uncle Loy's voice soft and hesitant but inflected with an edge of anger, a high-pitched voice overriding his gentler protests.

She felt a chill course over her skin as she recognized the voice. Tiredness faded as she hurried across the grass to see a familiar figure standing on the steps, yelling at Uncle Loy through the screen door.

Helen stole up on them, her steps muffled in the thick lawn. She didn't speak until she was right behind the intruder.

"Hello, Daddy."

Chapter Fourteen

Helen groped her way, aided by a flash of lightning, to a corner table. Yes, the candlestick stood just where she remembered it. She pawed the sides of the table until her fingers found a small knob. She pulled open the drawer and felt for a box of matches. In a moment the candle flickered into a thin flame and Helen could see her father perched on a chair.

Sitting on Aunt Ruth's old sofa in the living room, Helen watched in fascination as her father devoured his third cheeseburger. Helen herself had little appetite — the beers she'd consumed with Joe

Nathan had soured her stomach — and she'd given her own french fries to her father. He was smaller than she remembered. Thinner, too, with the painful hacking cough and barreled chest of emphysema. It was strange, and disturbing, to see a wasted and aging mirror of her own square, flat features chewing with evident enjoyment.

"Daddy —" The word came awkwardly to her lips, its unfamiliar shape pushing its way into the stale air of the empty house. He looked up, his jaw still working, and suppressed a belch. "I could have taken you to a restaurant, gotten you more of a real dinner than this."

He peered through the dust motes shifting in the gloom. "Nothin' wrong with this. I don't hold much with eatin' out, anyhow."

Helen realized it was his way of saying a grudging thanks for the food. She sighed and rattled the ice in her plastic cup and wished for another soft drink. "I guess I don't really understand why you wanted so much to see the place again, Daddy. I mean, you always hated Mama's family. Especially Aunt Ruth." She could still remember his voice, booming through the house, frightening her, as he railed at her mother about the awful ways of the McCormick clan. "And you know she left you nothing in her will," Helen added, impulsively stabbing at him with any weapon she could. She didn't like feeling sorry for the man who'd kicked her out of her own home, who'd refused to see her or talk to her or even to acknowledge her existence.

Except for the circular grinding of his jaws her father was motionless. The shadows hid his expression. He swallowed, then said, "Thought maybe you and me could have a talk. You know — catch up on things." His voice trailed off, as if even he realized how false his words sounded. "It ain't right for us to be strangers, Helen. I knew you was here for the funeral. Figured I'd maybe get a chance to talk to you, and then —"

"And then what?" Helen burst out, unable to contain her rage any longer. "All of a sudden we're going to be one big happy family again, is that it? Even though I'm still following my sinful ways?" But he wasn't really listening. "What the hell," she muttered. "I'm wasting my breath." She stood up and, carrying the candle, walked past her father to the kitchen, found a glass in the cupboard and turned on the faucet. As she did so, thunder rumbled close by. "Jesus Christ, doesn't it ever quit raining out here?"

"Storm coming in." She whirled around to find him standing just behind her. "Gonna hit us real soon."

"Then I'd better get you home," Helen said with relief. "The trailer park on the other end of town, right?"

Her words were submerged in a peal of thunder, closer now, and rain began pouring down as the rumbling faded. Water slammed against the windows and ceiling, roaring and punching against the wood and glass. Its intensity was startling, and Helen stared for several minutes at the sheets of water.

"Maybe we better wait until it lets up a little," her father said.

"Maybe so." Helen followed him back into the living room, where the stale smell of fried food hung in the air.

"Think I'll stretch out for a bit," he grunted. His face disappeared into the murk, and she stood holding the candle and listening to his heavy breathing.

"Like a heroine in some fucking horror movie," she said to herself, moving carefully through the house.

Back in the kitchen she found more candles rolling around in drawers next to tarnished silverware. Soon the kitchen looked like some sort of religious sanctuary, as candles glowed from every available surface. Restless, Helen wandered around the huge walk-in pantry behind the kitchen. A stack of moldering paperbacks, printed in the days when they cost a dime, was her only reward. Bemused, Helen turned them over until she saw one that boasted historical romance.

"Great. Bursting bodices." She settled herself at the kitchen table and tried to ignore the rain slashing outside. The heroine, suitably breathy and innocent, had just gotten off the boat on the stormy shores of England when Helen gave up and rested her head on her folded arms. The candles continued to burn while she slept, and the rain drummed lighter and lighter until it became only a faint pattering on the roof.

The grating sound coming from the back wall woke her a few minutes after one o'clock. She lifted her head to see all but the tallest candles worn down to puddles of soft wax. Behind her, outside, the eerie scraping continued — a slow methodical ringing of metal on stone that set her teeth on edge. What the hell —

Moonlight glowed through the parting clouds as

the rain died away. Still groggy with sleep, Helen stood up and peered out of the window. Yes, there was a figure there, hunched over and digging in the soft mud. It — she couldn't tell if it was male or female — must have been using a spade or shovel that would cause the rough grating sound that had awakened her.

The digging stopped, and she heard the clink of the spade being tossed aside. Something flat and square was lifted from the soil. Its dull surface reflected moonlight as it was wiped clean. Helen chose this moment, while the figure was absorbed in its discovery, to open the screen door and slip outside.

She stumbled in the mud as she caught up with the visitor near the end of Aunt Ruth's neglected vegetable garden. He — she could see now that it was a man — tripped over the brick-lined border that separated the garden from the woods. He fell with a painful grunt onto the overgrown weeds. Helen held him easily as he gasped for air, rolling over onto his back and turning his face into the soft white light from the full moon.

Her father panted, his face contorted with the effort to catch his breath. Helen sat back on her heels, ignoring the stray raindrops that pelted her shoulders. They stared at each other for a few moments, then he struggled to sit up. The flat metal box rested beside them on a mound of dead weeds that lay rotting in the moisture.

When she saw that he'd recovered from her flying tackle, Helen reached out with both hands to help him to his feet. She was shocked at his lightness, his lack of resistance. The man was really very sick.

"Daddy, what on earth are you doing?"

He pulled away and reached down to take up the box. "None of your business. This don't concern you, Helen."

"The hell it doesn't," she retorted, her anger returning. "This is my property, remember?" He was too weak to protest when she took the box away from him.

It was only after they had somewhat dried off with Aunt Ruth's towels and were sitting in the kitchen surrounded by a fresh batch of candles that he offered an explanation.

He gestured toward the box. "Your Aunt Ruth hid that away a few years back, when your grandpa first got sick. She ast me to come out here' and help her put it in the garden."

Helen, puzzled, stared at the box. "I don't get it, Daddy. Why did she want to hide this? What's in it?" She picked it up and examined its surface. The lid was rusted, clamped securely down. They'd need a screwdriver, at the very least, to pry it open. "And why would she want your help? You couldn't stand each other."

Even in the dim light she could see the smirk on his face. " 'Cause I helped build this house. I knew a few good places to hide things. Your grandpa was took sick, he couldn't do anything to help her. Besides, she paid me for it." His voice faded at the mention of his need, and Helen looked away, pained and guilt-ridden by his embarrassment.

To hide her feelings she got up and started poking around in the cabinets and drawers, hoping to come across some kind of tool that would enable them to open the box. "She didn't tell you what was in it, then?"

"Figured it was money, bonds, stuff like that." The words strained out reluctantly, and he kept his eyes averted. "Well, she didn't need it no more, did she? And no one knew about it but me. Nobody would ever miss it."

Helen barely heard his protests as she fished a screwdriver from a drawer by the sink. She grabbed one of the biggest candles from the window ledge and brought it over to the table. Her father moved his chair closer as she worked at the hinges of the lid, scraping away layers of dirt and rust as she prodded. The rain had completely stopped now, and the only sounds in the house were her father's labored breathing and the noise made by the screwdriver.

A cool breeze, following the edges of the storm, streamed through the kitchen and blew out a couple of candles as Helen pried the lid of the box open. She held her candle closer, feeling her father's breath on her neck as he leaned over her. Wordlessly she turned the box over and let its contents spill over the table.

Sitting back in surprise as she surveyed the items arrayed before her, Helen sighed. "We'd better take this stuff in to the police."

Chapter Fifteen

The connection was terrible. Helen could barely make out Frieda's anxious questions. "Are you sure I shouldn't come out there?" she was saying. "I called the airlines — I could be in Memphis by this afternoon."

Even though her lover's voice came through in patches, Helen could hear the tension over the line. It wasn't just concern for her safety. Did Frieda feel uneasy having Helen out of her sight? Helen stared out the window of the police station, trying to fight off her irritation at what felt like Frieda's smothering worry.

"Honestly, sweetheart, everything's fine. There's nothing to be upset about."

Helen leaned against the nearest desk, momentarily distracted by the sight of orange-vested men loading some kind of equipment into the back of a truck just outside the station. Two of them were talking to a uniformed officer. They looked anxiously over at the clouds gathering in the distance, and one officer gestured to his right, in the direction of the Big Black.

"What was that, Frieda? I didn't hear you." Silence followed, and Helen gave her attention back to the phone. "Frieda?"

"No, I guess you didn't hear me. You rarely do."

"Come on, Frieda —"

"It's obvious you just don't want me out there. Why? What is it you're not telling me?"

At that moment the phone line went dead. "Hello? Hello, Frieda?" Shit, Helen thought. What timing. She sighed and replaced the receiver, glancing out of the window in time to see the truck, tightly packed with equipment and road workers, pull away and head for the highway.

Beth looked up from her desk. "What's up?"

Helen shrugged. "Don't know. The phone just died on me."

Worry lines creased Beth's forehead. Helen noticed, for the first time that morning, how tight and dry her skin looked. Dark rings circled her eyes. "They've been up and down since the rain last night." She rubbed her face and leaned back in her chair, yawning. "We can't use the computers right now, either. Not to mention the roads either flooded or jammed with people heading north."

Helen sat opposite Beth. "What do you mean? What's going on?"

Beth stared in tired amazement. "The flood warnings. Haven't you heard? I guess you've been too busy to watch TV the last couple of days. We've got a possible flood situation on our hands." Beth regarded her with one of her enigmatic expressions. "Maybe you should think about getting out of Vicksburg for a few days. Go stay up with Edna and Loy."

Helen shook her head. "I can't just leave him, can I?" They both looked toward the narrow corridor where John Black lay stretched out on an uncomfortable bench, huffing and snorting.

Beth opened her mouth to protest, apparently thought better of it, and turned her gaze back to the items spread out on her desk. "Well, that tropical front is moving in from the gulf. Could be a hurricane." She fell silent as she brooded over the strange conglomeration from the box buried in the garden.

Helen shared her disappointment. The contents of the box her father had dug up revealed no hidden treasure of gilt-edged bearer bonds or precious gems or deeds to oil wells. He'd groaned out his dismay at the sight of a pile of letters, broken pencils, keys that didn't seem to fit anything, a roll of pennies and a few stray coins, a recipe card for cornbread stuffing, two postcards from New Orleans and a hopelessly outdated savings passbook.

"We even called up the bank where this is from,"

Beth said as she leafed idly through the pages of the passbook. "It doesn't exist any longer under this name. It got merged years ago with some other bank. And her account there was closed over ten years ago, anyway. Sorry."

Helen leaned over the desk, propping her aching head up on both hands. "Fuck. I thought maybe we'd find some clue in all this. Stupid of me."

"Helen, are you all right? It sounds like you haven't slept since you got here."

Beth's gentle touch on her hand sent a shock through her body, and Helen had vivid memories of their interlude the day before. The touch threatened to turn into a caress, and Helen was too hungry for it to shrug it off. Beth finally took her hand away with a glance around the empty room. "I think you'd better go somewhere and get some rest."

"You're right. I should go back to Aunt Edna's, unless —"

"You shouldn't be driving when you're so tired. You're coming back to my place."

"But — my father — the storm —"

"I have to stick it out for a few hours more. I'll make sure we get out of here in case we're told to evacuate." Beth suddenly smiled, and Helen felt warmth coursing through her tired bones. "Quit trying to be a tough dyke," Beth murmured. "Listen to someone else for a change."

Helen put Aunt Ruth's pitiful secret collection back in the box where it had been cached for so long. "She must have really been deteriorating badly, to want to save this kind of stuff."

Beth sighed and reached for her jacket. "Funny. Not so's you'd notice. I mean, to me she seemed sharp up to the very end." Beth turned to look at her. "Do you want to try calling Frieda again?"

Helen was saved from answering by the noise erupting from the hallway. John Black's voice rasped in the corridor, echoed by her cousin Maud's softer tones. Helen stepped out of the office, holding the box in her arms.

"Now, John, you know it's not going to be safe over in that trailer park! You'd better come on along with us," Maud was remonstrating.

"Damnfool woman, get your paws off me! Miss Goody Two Shoes, always tryin' to feed me and get me in church and take over my life! I said, get off me! I ain't one of your damn projects! And I'm more Christian than you'll ever be!"

Maud's face shone a deep red as she ushered Helen's father down the corridor. "We'll get you up to Arkansas, where it's safe," she said with a backward glance at Helen. Then Maud pointedly turned away, saying, "You don't want to be here all alone with her, do you? Not the kind of person she is."

Helen looked down as the sharp pain of rejection pierced her. Why did it still hurt so much? Her father, who'd always excoriated the McCormick family, was more welcome in Maud's home than she herself ever would be — even if his rescue from depravity was a lost cause. A blank cold feeling swept over her.

"Now what? You want to go home with me?" Beth asked. "Just say the word."

Helen regarded her for a moment before answering. "No, not yet. Do we have time to stop by the hospital?"

"Well, they may be making plans to evacuate the patients," Beth responded. "I'm sure your grandfather will be fine."

"No, it isn't that. I just need to talk to him for a moment."

Beth shrugged, grabbed her jacket and followed her outside. Beth paused by the car Helen had rented in Tupelo for the drive back to Vicksburg with her father. "I'll follow you there," she said, zipping up her jacket against the wind. "Might be as well to find out what the hospital plans to do."

Helen rolled down the car window. "You really think it might come to that? Evacuation?"

"People still talk about the flood of nineteen twenty-seven around here," Beth said. "Kind of like the big earthquake in San Francisco. Even with the levees and waterway stations, you know what a bitch that river can be."

Beth's mention of San Francisco brought Frieda back to Helen's mind. Maybe she'd go along to Jackson in hopes of calling Frieda from there before heading up to Aunt Edna's, with or without her grandfather. Corinth and Tupelo were far enough north to be safe, she thought. The sight of cars snaking down Highway 20 filled her with foreboding. By the time they reached the hospital, rain was lashing against the car window. The building's corridors were jammed with frantic patients and their families, but Beth's uniform ensured swift passage through the crowd. A strange silence enveloped the floor where her grandfather lay, and Helen took a deep breath before opening the door and facing those glittering eyes again.

Chapter Sixteen

Robert McCormick watched as the nurse adjusted yet another tube that led from his body to the complicated machinery at his side. It was ridiculous, of course, to imagine that he could be moved from the hospital under any circumstances. The ailing man waited until the nurse had left the room with one last disapproving glance at the intruders. Then he took a deep breath and spoke.

"I'll be just fine here, girls," he said. "Sweet of y'all to come and see an old goat like me."

Helen sat down on one of the chairs by the bed.

As she did so the metal box, which she'd been reluctant to leave behind in the car, slipped from her fingers. The rusted lid, which was bent because of Helen's jimmying earlier, popped open, and the contents fell in disarray across the white spread of the hospital bed.

"Oh, Lord, Grandpa, I'm sorry," Helen said as she scooped the things up from the bed and piled them back into the box.

"Where the hell — how'd you get those, child?"

Helen saw her grandfather's face freeze in horror at the sight of the pathetic pile of Aunt Ruth's possessions. "They're just some things I found over at Aunt Ruth's place. Why —"

Helen never finished her sentence. Bob McCormick's eyes blazed in his shrunken face, which quickly went from gray to startling white. High-pitched warnings began to whine from the monitoring equipment as he struggled to get words out. Horrified, Helen knelt by the bed, trying to understand.

Bony fingers clutched her arm with surprising strength. "Ruth," he gasped. Behind her Helen could hear Beth ushering two nurses toward the room. Her grandfather fixed his terrifying stare on Helen and moved his mouth in painful effort.

The harsh consonants he managed to blurt out confused her. It was a guttural choking that made no sense. Get? Get what? No, that wasn't it.

"Keep, Grandpa? You want me to keep the box?" Helen spoke over the shoulder of the doctor who had shoved her aside. That had to be it. Over and over again, the old man tried to say the word, "keep," even as he sank into breathless exhaustion.

Stunned, Helen stood in the hallway with Beth, imagining the huddled white-robed figures working over the dying man. After an excruciating few minutes the doctor came out, his face a study in carefully controlled anger.

"He's all right for now. I don't think this visit was the best idea, ladies." He looked accusingly at Beth. "You had some official reason for this?"

"Thank you, doctor," she replied. "We'll be in touch."

Once they'd left the corridor Helen found herself shaking. Could her grandfather have died in there?

"What the hell was that all about?" Beth asked as they walked to their cars. "Something about your aunt's stuff made him crazy."

"I think he was trying to tell me to keep the box. He kept saying 'keep, keep,' over and over again." Helen stood waiting as Beth sat down in the patrol car to radio in to the station. Unintelligible bleats came out of the speaker. Lost in thought, Helen barely noticed Beth's irritation as she got back out of the car.

"Shit. They want me back at the station." She fished in her pockets, then handed Helen a set of keys. "Why don't you go on over to my place for now? I'll get word to you as soon as I know what's up." Helen took the keys wordlessly. "You remember how to get there?"

Only after Helen's repeated assurances did Beth speed off back to the station. Helen took a few steps to her own car, then abruptly turned back to the hospital. She found a remote telephone in a quiet corner of the first floor. A couple of phone calls finally garnered her some helpful information.

"Yes, ma'am, we used to be the old First National Bank of Vicksburg," the elderly woman drawled into Helen's ear. "Let's see, now — when was that? Well, about ten years ago we got bought out by Delta Bank, and it was quite a mess, I can tell you —"

"Ten years ago?" Helen interrupted. The last entry in the passbook hoarded by Aunt Ruth was dated September 9, 1965. Helen wasn't sure how much information the bank would give her over the phone. While the sweet, motherly voice droned on, she frowned, waiting for an opportunity to speak. When the bank clerk finally drew a breath, Helen asked, "Where are you located?" Helen scribbled hastily on a scrap of paper she'd dug up from inside a pocket. "Clay Street?"

"Yes, ma'am, out by the old County Courthouse. Y'all know where that is?"

Helen clearly remembered it — the tidy, simple building built by slaves before the Civil War, now a museum of dead dreams, guarded by cannon that faced out toward the river. She could recall standing by the cannon, waiting for her grandfather to emerge from the new courthouse. He was still the sheriff for Warren County then.

"I'll be able to find it," she said.

She steered the car unerringly through the narrow streets of the downtown district, moving cautiously through the heavy rain. Once or twice she got a glimpse of the river roiling thick and muddy under the iron-colored sky. As she got out and hurried through the door of First National, Helen felt the emptiness of the city. It appeared as if most of the downtown shops had closed up in anticipation of evacuating the area, and the few cars she'd passed had been speeding in the direction of Highway 20.

The young black man who invited her to sit down seemed nervous. The nameplate on his desk informed her that he was the assistant manager of the branch.

"Sorry about the commotion," he said after shaking her hand. "We've just got word form the police that we need to close up and leave."

Helen looked around at the scurrying figures carrying heavy files and trundling rollaway carts into the cavernous vault at the other end of the room. "Well, I appreciate your time, Mr. Pilkington. This shouldn't take too long." She pulled the passbook from her bag and explained, leaving out the details of her father's excavation of Aunt Ruth's grounds. Mr. Pilkington's large dark eyes stared at her evenly from behind his gold-rimmed glasses, assessing both Helen and her story.

He cleared his throat and drummed his fingers on the desk. "Quite honestly, Ms. Black, I'm under a legal obligation to keep all records confidential. I do understand your position — I recall now seeing Ms. McCormick's obituary." He paused, looked at her as if trying to make up his mind about something, then shook his head gently. "Normally we require court papers showing you to be the executor of the estate before we can release any information at all."

Helen watched him intently. There was something else going on here — why was he studying her so hard? Surely these were routine questions that any surviving relative would ask a bank official.

Someone coughed, and Helen turned to see a very young, very pretty blonde standing behind her, twisting her manicured hands and smiling nervously.

"Yes, Michelle?"

"I'm really sorry, Mr. Pilkington —"

"It's all right, Michelle. What's up?"

"Well, we were just about to lock up the vault, and we were wondering if we could close the doors and get ready to leave." The girl nervously glanced at the doors as a bolt of lightning jagged across the blackened sky.

"Of course, Michelle. Everyone get all their cash locked up?" He pushed his chair back from the desk and stood up, his height barely reaching five feet. He looked apologetically at Helen. "I'm terribly sorry —"

Helen fought to conceal her disappointment. "I understand. I won't keep you any longer. Perhaps I could come back in a day or so."

As he shook her hand again he seemed to come to some sort of decision about her. He burst out, "I think I can go as far as telling you that the account is still open." Helen waited for more, but he looked away. Taking one of his business cards from the holder on his desk, he jotted something on the back of the card and handed it to her. "This is my home phone number," he said, turning his serious brown gaze back to her. "Give me a call, here or at home as soon as things calm down. I'd like to talk to you about your aunt."

Mystified, Helen allowed herself to be shepherded out the door, which clattered behind her as keys were turned in the heavy bolts. What could Pilkington possibly know about Aunt Ruth?

Frustrated, Helen turned back down Clay Street.

She thought she remembered the side road that led out to the access road. If she was right, Beth's place lay only a few blocks on the other side of that road. The orange-striped barriers at the end of the side street elicited a few muttered curses from Helen. As she backed out onto Clay Street again thunder shook the air. For the first time she began to really worry. Maybe she ought to go by the station instead, find out what Beth was up to. Any attempt to get the legal documentation necessary for the bank to proceed would certainly be futile today. She could always head back up to Tupelo, but she didn't like leaving Beth stranded down here.

A black-and-white patrol car, lights flashing, interrupted her thoughts. It blocked the entrance to an auto repair shop near Clay. The grimy gray building seemed to ooze black moisture from its walls, and the downpour sheeted over the derelict vehicles that littered the pavement. One hunched figure skulked out into the rain toward the police car, guided none too gently by a uniformed escort. Helen slowed down long enough to see the scowling face of Don Watson staring at her through the rain.

Chapter Seventeen

No one paid much attention to Helen as she hung back quietly in a corner of the station. Beth had given her a swift look and a nod, then merged with the crowd gathered inside the sheriff's office. A cluster of reporters milled around the front desk, firing questions at the uniformed policewoman standing there.

"Look, folks, I don't have any information for y'all yet. We have picked up two suspects for questioning — but you'll just have to wait for the rest of it."

In the general clamor that followed her announcement, a slight elderly man made his way around the edge of the crowd. His arthritic hands trembled at his sides, and Helen could see his fear as he passed by. The officer at the desk looked at him in recognition. She beckoned him forward, and instantly the reporters were on him.

He shrugged his way past them, cowering under their shouted questions as if warding off physical blows. With exasperated groans the representatives of the press watched him being shuffled down the corridor toward the room where Don was being questioned.

"And who the hell is that?"

"He's not with the police, is he?"

"Never saw him before. How'd he get in?"

The room buzzed with curiosity. Helen thought that the man had looked vaguely familiar, but she couldn't quite place him. One of the reporters standing near her muttered a name. Several people stopped talking to listen. The man was older than most of the crowd. His gray hair and tired eyes told of years in the reporting trade, and he seemed bored with the whole business.

"Hal Watson. The kid's uncle."

"Of course," Helen breathed to herself. It came back to her in a rush — her grandfather's best friend. They'd gone fishing together, hunted together, walked the beat together for years. It was Hal Watson's face that beamed out at the camera from the old photograph in the hospital. A chill shot through the rush of memory as she realized that they'd even planned and built Aunt Ruth's house together. She tugged at her thoughts for more information. Hadn't

Hal taken Don in when the boy's parents had died in the car accident? Everyone had been so astonished that Hal would let his nephew run around with such a wild crowd, predicting he'd come to no good.

Lost in concentration, Helen was startled when Beth appeared by her side. "His uncle got him a lawyer," she said. "They'll probably set bail pretty high."

"I saw Hal Watson go in," Helen said. No one seemed to be paying them any attention. All eyes were turned to the corridor, where Hal and his nephew were being ushered toward the doors. Helen noted with surprise that the handcuffs had been removed from Don's wrists, and his arms swung free as he swaggered, surrounded by nervous officers. His bright red work shirt, emblazoned with his name in white script over the words LAST CHANCE AUTO, was torn at the shoulder. The loose flap of the sleeve bounced as he strode along the hallway.

Beth shook her head and sighed. "Hal started bitching and moaning about the handcuffs. Can you believe this? There's still a lot of good ol' boys here that respect his poor injured feelings, so they took them off."

The two women trailed after the newshounds who buzzed like insects around the Watsons, while Don's less fortunate sidekick sulked on the sidelines, his hands still bound behind his back. Beth and Helen stood near the steps, watching Don enjoy his moment of fame.

"What was the connection to Don?" Helen asked.

"All those tire tracks. Remember, there were different ones at each site? It all clicked when we found out that each of those cars had been in the auto repair shop where Don works. He'd just switch a couple of tires around while the cars were in the shop, go out with his buddies, come back and switch tires again. After tying it up with three of the cars, we got a warrant to search the shop. Came up with a couple of bits and pieces off Don's car —"

"Let me guess. Fabric from the victim's clothes."

Beth, startled, glanced at her. "Right."

Helen kept her eyes fixed on the sky. Lightning cracked across the blackness and thunder followed, reverberating over the city spread before them. Rain lashed down into their faces with a sharp slap. The reporters bent under the downpour tried to gather themselves for more questions, finally gave up. The crowd fragmented and dispersed toward various vehicles.

"Now what?" Helen asked.

"They're going to take him over to Jackson," Beth answered. "In fact, they'll probably empty out the cells here, load everybody on the bus and take them all over there." As she spoke, she took Helen's arm and led her back into the station. "I think you should get out of here, too. Why don't you stop by my place, pick up some things for us both and head up to Tupelo, up to Loy and Edna's place? I can meet you up there as soon as things settle down here."

Shielded from the driving rain by the metal awning, Helen smiled up at Beth. "Giving orders again. Maybe it's wearing a uniform. It makes you think you can take over."

Beth was still holding Helen's arm as she said, "You don't sound like you're complaining about it."

"How long do you think you'll need to stay here?"

"Who knows? We're going to have to get the word out, fast, that people need to get moving. The reports from the gulf make it sound like we're in for a hurricane, maybe in just a few hours." She glanced back at the van where Don Watson still held court with a few intrepid journalists. "I've got to head out to —"

She cut her words short. An odd smell, something like hot metal, sliced through the rain. Instinctively Helen grabbed Beth, as if her protective gesture could ward off the danger from the lightning that extended a thin white finger from the sky to the earth. Blue and white sparks flared from the surface of a station wagon that sported the logo of a local news program on its side. The arc's brief life sizzled into foul-smelling smoke that died quickly as thunder echoed all around them. The sudden flash had momentarily blinded everyone. A couple of seconds ticked by before Helen saw the man lying on the ground next to the station wagon. He was still twitching in spasmodic jerks, eyes and mouth wide open. A uniformed officer bent over him. Another officer rushed past Beth and Helen into the station, no doubt to call for paramedics.

Beth and Helen hurried toward the crowd.

"Come on, people, let's give them some room," Beth said.

Few responded to her request. Most stood staring down at their colleague, who lay motionless beneath the thin blanket that had been grabbed from the trunk of a black-and-white and tossed onto the ground. Helen hung behind, watching the others. The parking lot and the station house were both completely dark. Helen glanced around uneasily.

There was no light coming from beyond the incline to her right, where Vicksburg lay spread out by the river. The only illumination came from brief flashes of lightning, which came far too close for comfort,

Beth appeared at her side. "We're gonna have to get you out of here."

"And you?" Helen resisted as Beth tried to guide her back in the direction of her rented car, which was parked in a visitor's space around the side of the building. "Now what? I'm supposed to leave you here to drown or get electrocuted?" Immediately Helen hated herself for the fear and concern that she knew rang in her voice.

Beth ignored the rain that pelted them both and rested her hands on Helen's shoulders. They were alone, away from the throng still gathered around the station wagon. "Sounds like maybe you give a damn what happens to me, Helen."

Before Helen could come up with a rejoinder, she felt herself in the warm circle of Beth's arms. The brief embrace left Helen shaken. "Careful," she tried to joke. "Someone might catch us. Think of your reputation."

"Fuck it," Beth whispered. A quick burst of hot, humid air bathed them as the rain abated. Beth raised a hand to Helen's cheek and left it there in a light caress. They broke apart when voices approached. "Get going," Beth said with a smile.

Helen had just started the engine and turned on the headlights and windshield wipers when Don suddenly appeared around the side of the building, his hair plastered to his forehead, the red shirt wet and shining from the rain. Although it took only two seconds, Helen saw what followed as if it happened under deep waters, the action slowed and refracted before her eyes. Beth was backing away from the car, still smiling, when Don lunged forward and struck her on the back of her head. Helen sprang from the car, but Don already had Beth's gun in his hand.

He grinned as he leveled the barrel at her. "Shit," he said with a giggle. "I just got me a one-way ticket out of this toilet."

Two other officers, guns drawn, hurtled around the corner and stopped short at the sight of Beth, struggling up from the wet asphalt, and Don, holding the gun to Helen's head.

With a curious indifference Helen felt the cool kiss of metal against her temple. She automatically registered its weight, the man's strength, and the slim chances she had of knocking him on his fat ass.

Don was breathing heavily. Stale body odor filled Helen's nostrils. His breath smelled of Jack Daniel's. "Come on. You too," he said to Beth. "We're going to take us a little tour. The scenic route."

Beth edged cautiously toward the car, her eyes fixed on Don. Behind her the two cops stirred. "You don't need her," Beth said with a glance at Helen. "Two is one too many. You'll have your hands full with me. Let her go, and —"

"Shut up, you fuckin' cunt," he hissed. Helen turned away from the weird glitter in his eyes.

"Don, this'll only get you in deeper. You know that." Beth slid onto the back seat, wincing as she bumped her head against the door frame.

The gun nudged sharply into Helen's temple when he slammed the door shut. "Keep it up and the bitch's brains are gonna be all over the wheel."

Beth subsided as Helen backed the car out.

Scurrying figures darted around the station house in the wake of their departure.

"Go to Highway Twenty," Don ordered.

Helen allowed herself a look at Beth in the rearview mirror. Their eyes met for a moment, then Helen turned her attention to the road.

Chapter Eighteen

Helen gripped the steering wheel tightly. She wanted to make sure her hands were in plain sight. Meanwhile her mind raced. The silence inside the car was excruciating. She stared out the windshield through sheets of rain at the Big Black. Don had ordered her to stop on the side of the road. Rain lashed against the car, and the wind was picking up. She could hear Don's heavy breathing, smell the stench of his fear.

"Shit," he muttered. "Shit." The hand holding the

gun trembled, and he kept rocking back and forth in the seat. "Man, oh man."

Helen shifted slightly, turning so that she could watch his face. Was it safe to talk? "We can't stay here much longer, Don," she said quietly.

"Shut up, bitch!" Helen checked her recoil at the sight of the gun's barrel waving at her. "Lemme figure this thing out without you fuckin' it up."

Once again Helen met Beth's eyes in the mirror. If Don was rattled enough to admit to his confusion, then maybe they had a chance to talk their way out of this thing without getting hurt.

"Don," Beth began, "you know they're going to be right behind us. You don't have a chance of getting away. Why make it worse?"

He glared at her for a couple of seconds. "And what do you figure my chances are now, cunt? If they catch me now they'll fry me in Parchman for sure, along with all them niggers."

"You don't know that, Don." Beth continued her calm, quiet efforts to distract him, giving Helen a chance to gauge the difficulty of getting the gun away from him. "Maybe you just need a chance to tell everyone about what really happened. Why you did it."

Don's laugh came out as a high-pitched squeal. "Why? What the hell are you—a fuckin' shrink? Them bitches needed killin'—just a bunch of damn monkeys, always cryin' about their rights and their dignity. Things used to be different. People knew who they were. Now they even got some black whore workin' at the garage. Christ, what the fuck is goin' on in America these days?"

His political diatribe kept him from paying

attention to the thunder that roared outside the car. Helen released the wheel, ignored the pain in her tense fingers, and let her right hand slowly drop to the seat. She'd have to be fast.

"And what would you know about it, pussy-licker? You're so busy eatin' out your girlfriends you don't see what's happenin'. The shit is gonna come down right on your bulldyke face."

While he spoke lightning struck a metal fence post a few feet in front of the car. The chain-link fence separating the road from the river spit out light and wisps of flame that dissolved in the rain. The smell of ozone drifted into the car.

"Wha—" He didn't get a chance to finish.

Helen landed her fist directly into his face while he was still dazzled by the flash. The fingers of her right hand clawed at his eyes, and her left slammed his arm against the dashboard with a satisfying crack. The gun went off, shattering the windshield. Broken glass shimmered across the hood of the car. The blast from the gun broke Helen's timing, and she relaxed her grip on Don's face for one second.

It was all he needed. He screamed and shoved her against the steering wheel. By now the gun was nowhere in sight, and Helen gasped in pain as he banged her head on the wheel. There was a brief break in the pressure as Beth lunged forward and yanked Don's head back, pulling at his hair. He shouted and loosened his grip on Helen. She fought to stay conscious, her head starting to ring with pain. Before her vision had cleared, she felt cold water spray across her face as Don ducked out of Beth's hammerlock and flung himself out of the car.

Helen and Beth ran after him, slipping through

the mud and rain until they reached the river's edge where Don stood, cursing and gingerly holding his injured arm. Silhouetted against the lightning that streamed across the sky, his body contrasted sharply with the surging black water that rushed past his feet.

The two women had almost reached him when Helen saw the muzzle of the gun pointing at them, its smooth black cylinder shimmering as it shook in his good hand.

"Get ready, you fuckin' cunts," he yelled. "I'm gonna blow your brains out all over the river!"

Beth grabbed Helen and managed to shove her aside behind her own body. "Don, look!" she shouted. He turned and squinted toward the flashing lights in the distance. "There's no way you'll make it now. If you kill us, you're sure to get the chair in Parchman, and —"

"What the fuck, bitch? I'm gonna get it now for riddin' the world of a few niggers." Still wielding the gun, he looked out across the river. "Things got all fucked up by those bleeding-hearts way back when. Uncle Hal should've finished what they started."

"No, Don." The sonorous voice pierced through the storm. Startled, Helen jerked away from Beth and turned to see Hal Watson standing beside the car, balancing a shotgun in his withered hands.

"Drop that gun, now."

Don's face relaxed into hope at the sight of his uncle. "See what happened?" He lowered the gun and took a step closer to the old man, Helen and Beth momentarily forgotten. "It all turned out just like you said — niggers and homos takin' over everything, while men like us lose it all."

Helen's eyes locked on Hal Watson as Don stumbled up from the bank. The old man seemed intent on his nephew, barely registering the presence of the two women. She felt the tension in Beth's body and was sure that they were both calculating the difficulty of getting the gun away from Don.

The shotgun didn't budge. "It's too late, son. We can't stop 'em. The past is dead and gone."

Don froze. "Uncle Hal?" he whimpered. "What are you talkin' 'bout? You gone nuts? There's a dozen guys right now I could get to —"

Helen leaped forward, grabbed his arm and snapped it back so that the gun flew out of his grasp. She heard the faint splash as it landed in the river behind them. Don screamed out in pain and anger as Helen and Beth fought him down to the ground.

Fear and rage pushed Don into a frenzy of motion. His face contorted, he struggled free of Beth's tenuous grasp. At the same moment Helen reeled back from a violent shove and slipped in the mud. For the space of two or three seconds Don was free, his arms flailing, his face turned to his uncle.

The blast from the shotgun dazzled Helen. She slid down again, flat on the earth, rain and wind hammering her shoulders and back with painful force. A quick glance to her left reassured her that Beth was unhurt. She lay prone, her eyes huge and glittering.

Don had fallen to his knees. A bright red stain spread quickly across his back, like some deadly flower in rapid bloom. He had to be dead before he finally fell to the ground. The dull thud of his corpse landing in the mud seemed to Helen to reverberate in the thunder that enveloped them. Through the sounds of the storm Helen heard the approach of the police, sirens blasting and tires whining as they sped up the road.

"Helen —" Beth croaked. Helen looked up again and saw that Beth was kneeling by the body. Her shirt was stained with blood that turned purple beneath the rain. It was the last thing Helen saw before she slipped into soothing darkness.

Chapter Nineteen

Helen sipped at her coffee and watched the sun crest over the tops of the trees behind Loy and Edna's trailer. Aside from the occasional burst of wind that shook water from the branches, there was no evidence here in Tupelo of the tropical storm that had ravaged Mississippi farther south. Beth and Uncle Loy sat at the table with her, while Edna busied herself with the pan of eggs frying on the stove.

"And not one reporter called since she got here," Loy said to Beth. "Good thing you got her up to us as fast as you did, or they would've been all over her like fleas on a dog."

"When did they find Hal Watson?" Helen asked, keeping her gaze on the distant trees.

Beth cleared her throat. "While they were taking us to the hospital, one of the patrol cars followed Hal's truck. He kept going back through those woods around the river, didn't pay any attention to the police at all."

Edna tut-tutted while she set a plate heaped with bacon and eggs and biscuits before Helen. "I've known Hal since he worked with your grandpa," she sighed. "I just can't believe he'd kill that nephew of his, no matter how much Don deserved it. Go on, now, eat up, darlin'. You must be starved."

Helen savored the salty, greasy bacon as she listened to Beth.

"Didn't take long before Hal had wrapped that truck around a tree. They said he died instantly, probably didn't feel a thing," Beth finished quickly.

They all sat in silence for a few minutes, the quiet broken only by the scrape of Helen's fork against the plate. Helen knew they were all thinking the same thing—that it would always be a question of whether or not Hal had deliberately aimed his truck at the tree, not wanting to face what lay ahead of him.

Helen looked back out of the window at her cousin Bobby, who was busily patting mud into some shape that only he understood. He looked up, saw Helen, gave her a brilliant smile, then bent back to his mysterious work. "And what about Bobby?"

"The sheriff wants him to testify at the trial of those other men who were in on it." Loy reached out to take his wife's hand. "I guess they never thought anyone would listen to him. Not to mention how they scared him to death, tellin' him they'd hurt him like those poor girls." His face reddened with anger and one hand twisted at his ear with suppressed rage.

Edna's eyes once again filled with tears. "Lord knows I try to be a good Christian, but all I can say is that those boys deserve everything they get."

"Considering that most of the population at Parchman is black, I'd say they're in for quite a time, whether or not they get the chair." Beth glanced at Helen. "Some things never change, do they?"

Edna got up from the table and started washing dishes in the sink while Loy mumbled something about fixing a backhoe. He slipped his cap over his head and left the women in the house. Helen looked up at her empty plate to find Beth smiling at her.

"Better?" Beth asked.

"Believe it or not, I've eaten more real food in the last week than I have in years. Probably added a few inches, too."

"You look fine to me." Helen blushed as Beth's stare intensified. Beth pushed away from the table. "Guess I'd best get back to Vicksburg, see if anything's still standing."

"Mind if I hitch a ride? I should probably do the same with Aunt Ruth's place."

"No problem."

"Aunt Edna? Do you mind?" Helen stood behind her aunt and put an arm around the plump shoulders. "I can be back up by tomorrow."

"You go right ahead, hon. What should I tell those realtors if they call about the house?"

"Tell them —" Helen hugged her again. "Tell them I've changed my mind. I have other plans for the house."

"You mean, you're not going to sell it?" Beth looked puzzled.

Edna turned around to plant a loud kiss on Helen's cheek. "When you get back we can have a real good visit, without anything to get in the way."

Helen stopped Beth when they reached the front door. "I just want to try one more time to reach Frieda."

"I — uh — I talked to her yesterday."

"You what?"

Beth looked away from Helen. "She called while you were still out of it, Helen. She was scared to death about you, so I just told her you were okay."

"That's all?"

"That's all."

Helen watched Beth, unsure of what she should be feeling.

"She sounds like a good person, Helen."

"She is. Especially to put up with me for so long."

"And she sounds like she loves you very much." With her back to the door, Beth was cast in shadow so Helen couldn't read her face. "Did you ever tell her about me?"

Helen shook her head. "It always seemed to be so much in the past for me, Beth. I'd cut all that away from me. Or so I thought. I wanted to completely forget where I'd come from, to bury it under a whole new life in California."

Beth chuckled and leaned against the wall. When she moved, Helen could once again see her face, see the smile that played around her lips and eyes. "Nothing ever goes away, as any shrink worth his or her salt would tell you. The things you think you get over — you never really do. Like, I'm not sure how much I'm over you."

"Beth —"

"Go ahead and try the phone," Beth said, reaching for the door. "I'll just say good-bye to Loy," and the screen door slammed behind her.

Helen watched her walk across the grass toward the work shed before she picked up the phone from the table by the door. She sighed in irritation when the recorded voice told her that all lines were busy due to the recent storm. Of course, across the country people were desperately trying to find out if loved ones had safely survived the hurricane's passage into the Gulf of Mexico. Helen hung up before the recording advised her to try again later. At least Frieda knew, thanks to Beth, that she was all right.

Helen had settled in Beth's car before Beth emerged from the work shed. "All set?"

"Ready." For the long drive back to Vicksburg they carefully talked about Don Watson, the storm, Bobby, her grandfather — anything besides the emotions that lay dormant between them. It was only when Beth finally pulled into her driveway that Helen allowed herself to realize what was going to happen.

"Storm's coming," Beth said as they went inside. "Just a leftover from yesterday, I think."

Helen stood uncertainly in the living room while Beth checked the outside of the house for damage. She tried the light switch. No luck. Great.

"You still don't have power," she said when Beth came back in.

"I'll get the fire going."

Helen couldn't take her eyes off Beth as she knelt before the fireplace and coaxed flames from the wood. The flickering light glowed on her skin, lit her eyes and stole in and out of her hair. Without a word Helen knelt behind Beth and stroked her shoulders.

"Helen, are you sure you want to do this?" Beth whispered as she leaned back into Helen's hand.

"Yes," Helen murmured, her lips brushing Beth's neck. The sharp intake of Beth's breath excited her even more, and her hands found Beth's breasts as she kept her mouth on Beth's neck. Soon Beth was lying down by the fire while Helen stretched on top of her. Their mouths sought each other hungrily.

"What about Frieda?" Beth asked as Helen began to unbutton her shirt.

"Frieda isn't here. This is just you and me, Beth." Beth moaned, stroking Helen's hair as Helen's tongue traveled between her breasts. "Just you and me," Helen whispered again.

There were no more words as Helen slowly spread Beth's legs apart. Sweat glistened in the firelight on Beth's skin as she cried out in pleasure. Helen watched her face as she relaxed with a sigh.

Swiftly Helen rose up, turned and straddled Beth as she lay on the floor. Beth searched for and found Helen's soft, wet warmth with her lips. Outside the rain drummed on the roof as Helen moaned and shuddered. They curled up in front of the fire, listening to the rain and their own breathing.

"Helen."

"What?"

"What the hell are we doing?"

"Hey, I'm the one who's supposed to do the agonized soul-searching, remember?" Helen nudged her gently. "You're the free spirit throwing caution to the winds. Let's stick to our roles."

Beth chuckled, sat up and reached for another log to put on the fire. Helen traced her spine with her fingertips. Beth stayed sitting where she was.

Helen felt suddenly cold. "Beth, are you sorry about this?"

Beth turned around. "No." She leaned back and kissed Helen tenderly. "No. I'm afraid that you will be in a little while."

Helen circled her arms around Beth's shoulders, pulling her down on top of her. "We're big girls now, Beth," she said. "We're not in high school anymore. We've both had our hearts broken once or twice. I think we can weather this, too."

"Maybe." Beth's tongue moved from Helen's wrist across her arm. They kissed passionately. "We can put on a good show, at least." Beth's body pushed against Helen's with increasing pressure as they fell silent again.

Later, while Beth slept under a blanket by the fireplace, Helen pulled on her clothes and stood at a window. The rain had stopped, and she could see the moon, huge and close, hovering over the house. By its light she could read her watch — two-thirty. Better try to get some sleep before going into action that day. She had an idea she'd need all the rest she could get.

Chapter Twenty

Ray Pilkington accepted the glass of iced tea from Helen. "Thanks." He swallowed long and hard. Helen filled her own glass from the thermos she'd brought to the house on Pemberton Road. She could see beads of sweat on the smooth dark skin of his neck as he tilted his head back. "That's really good."

Helen sat on Aunt Ruth's sofa, across the room from him. "Hard to believe that storm went through here, isn't it? It's so hot today." The sun blazed outside. There was no breeze to stir the tall grass that grew unchecked just beyond the porch. "I want to thank you for coming out here to talk to me."

"No problem. I did give you my number. In fact, I was sort of hoping you'd call." He swirled his tea, making the ice cubes clink against the glass. "How well did you know your Aunt Ruth?" he asked suddenly.

Helen was surprised at the question. "Not well at all, actually. I — I left Mississippi when I was eighteen. In fact, I couldn't believe she left this house to me." There was a long pause. "Why do you ask?"

In answer, Ray got up and crossed the room to sit next to her, pulling a wallet from his back pocket. "I want to show you something," he said, flipping through credit cards and photographs. "Here."

She looked down at the black and white snapshot. An elderly black man with grizzled white hair, spectacles and a dignified air stared back at her.

"My grandfather," Ray was saying. "This photograph was taken back in nineteen sixty-three. He died in seventy-three. Eighty years old."

Helen smiled. "You look a lot like him."

Ray sighed and put the wallet back in his pocket. "He was the first Raymond Pilkington. In those days he was a preacher at the African United Methodist Church, over on the other end of Culkin Road."

"I remember him!" Helen said. "That's just about a mile from here. He was pretty famous — the soup kitchen, the college fund, the free clinic."

Ray got up and paced around the room, his hands stuffed into his pockets. "That's right. He did an awful lot of good for the community. Lots of people around here still remember that." He paused and looked down at her. "But all those projects cost money. Strange, isn't it, how the poorest segment of society in the poorest state in the country came up with the money for such things?"

Helen stared at him warily. What was he getting at? "Well, I'm no expert on state history, but —"

"Think about it." He still spoke softly, but his stare unnerved her. "Nothing changed overnight. Medgar Evers got killed in sixty-three, the march in Selma was two years later, then of course Dr. King in Memphis, nineteen sixty-eight."

"All right, Ray. All of that's true. Where is this going?"

Ray sat down and picked up his glass, drained it and set it on the floor carefully. "Before my grandfather died, I went to visit him. I was starting at Ole Miss in a couple of months, and I went to see him at the rest home before going up to Oxford. He told me how he got the money for all those community programs." Ray cleared his throat, clasped his hands together. "It was from Ruth McCormick."

"Aunt Ruth." Helen took the news quietly, not sure what to think.

"She sold off a lot of land back around the late fifties. Got a good price for it. She'd set up a trust account for Granddaddy, as well as giving him a lot of cash from the sale." He leaned back in the chair. "That's how he was able to do all that."

"But no one knew about any of this?" Helen asked.

"She told him never, ever to tell a soul about it. It was to be their secret. Granddaddy said she got furious with him whenever he wanted her to get credit. He figured it was because of her brother being the sheriff. Wouldn't look too good for his family to be helping out all the coons, would it?" Ray said, a bitter smile twisting his lips.

They sat in silence for a while, then Helen finally said, "Why are you telling me this, Ray?"

He reached down and pulled a long, narrow object out of his briefcase, then handed it to her. It was a safety deposit box. At one end of the hinged lid was an old-fashioned lock, still gleaming and rust-free.

"When the bank was bought out, all the customers were given new safe deposit boxes once we were remodeled. All except your aunt. By then she was far gone — couldn't recognize anybody, hardly knew her own name. So I broke some major rules and took this home. Since she hadn't paid rent on it for several years, they'd end up forcing it open and looking through her things." He shrugged. "I figured she ought to have this without a lot of hassle and red tape."

Helen held the box in her lap and looked at him. "You have no idea what's in here?" she asked as she fiddled with the lock.

He shook his head. "Granddaddy broke his promise by telling me about her money, but he wanted someone to know before he died. He said —"

"What did he say?"

"He said it must've been blood money. His words, exactly." Suddenly he leaned down, grabbed his briefcase and headed for the door. "I've already told you more than I've ever told anyone about all this. Including my wife." He paused, one hand holding the screen door open. "I know what's been going on at this house lately, Ms. Black — the body, Watson and his gang. And I know your grandfather's dying.

Maybe what's in this box will get the truth out at last."

Helen stood up, still clutching the box. "Don't you want to know what's in it?"

He was already at his car. Tossing his briefcase onto the back seat, he turned and shook his head. "I figure she left you her house — you have a right to all her things. Including whatever you find in there."

Helen watched him as he revved the engine. "Wait," she called out, approaching the car. He rolled his window down, and she put out her hand. "Since you've confessed breaking the law to me, I guess you can at least call me Helen."

He grinned, shook her hand, then drove off down Pemberton Road in a cloud of dust. The dirt settled slowly in the afternoon heat, leaving a gritty film on Helen's skin and clothes. Slowly she turned back to the house and made her way to the kitchen. The recently discovered grave in the backyard had been washed level by the storm, the yellow tape markers swept away. Helen debated pouring herself a shot of Aunt Ruth's hoarded bourbon, then decided against it.

"No time like the present," she said aloud.

The key fit smoothly into the lock and the lid lifted without a squeak of protest. Helen took a deep breath and began removing the contents, laying them neatly on the table. Letters, newspaper clippings about local events, a scrap of cloth caught in the hinge, a few pieces of costume jewelry, an envelope containing Confederate bills from God knew where. Helen went quickly through the letters, hoping for enlightenment, but was disappointed almost as soon as she started. One contained a recipe for pecan pie. Another was from the lumber leasing company that had purchased her land. There were a couple of bills from local contractors who had worked on building her house. Nothing else.

Maybe bourbon was a good idea, after all. Helen found a glass and poured herself a liberal helping. God, it was hot. For the first time in several days she thought of Berkeley, which even in the summer had fog from the bay bathing the city with its cool moist air. Her mind wandered to Frieda — then on to Beth. She finished the bourbon and sat down gloomily at the table.

"Shit," she muttered. "Not a goddamned thing here."

The bourbon began to take hold of her. Idly she amused herself by flipping the lid of the box up and down with her finger, watching the scrap of cloth move back and forth, back and forth. That's what it's like with me and Frieda, Helen thought. Back and forth. Never just happy with each other. And what about Beth? She would never tell Frieda about it, but the fact that she'd eagerly made love to her high school sweetheart would always linger in the back of her mind. Maybe it was all that old-time religion drilled into her at a young age. She just couldn't get away from the feelings of guilt over her lack of perfection, even though she knew Frieda would love her in spite of her recent episode of unfaithfulness. Or would she? Was Helen counting on Frieda's patience too much?

Back and forth. She sighed as she piled everything back into the box. Another shot of bourbon and she'd be ready to go get something to eat. Helen pondered what might tempt her appetite in this heat as she stood up.

As she set down the safe deposit box filled with memories of an old woman she felt a sudden wave of sadness, made worse by Ray's comments on how terrible the situation had been in Mississippi when she was born. Why hadn't she seen any of it when she was growing up? Not just the social ostracizing, but the brutality and violence. The kind of perverted thinking that led to the creation of a Don Watson. Not that the South had a monopoly on cruelty, of course. It was just depressing to know that one's heritage included the ugly face of racism.

She stood at the screen door, lost in thought. Heat waves shimmered over the grass in a surge of greenish gold. The bourbon was hitting her in a big way because she hadn't eaten much. Still she lingered, puzzling over something in the back of her mind. What was it?

When the idea surfaced she went back to the sofa and opened the safe deposit box again. Yes, she was sure she was right. Helen gazed into the box for a long time before leaving the house.

Chapter Twenty-One

Helen shut the hospital door behind her and looked anxiously down at her grandfather. The doctor had allowed her this special visit on the condition that she keep it short and didn't allow him to get excited. She wasn't sure how much time she'd need, but it would all be pointless if he was going to remain unconscious.

Just as she was wondering if she should risk rousing him his eyes flickered open and glittered up at her. Strange how all his energy seemed to be concentrated in those dark circles burning in his face. He didn't speak, even when she pulled a chair up close to the bed.

"Hello," she said softly. "The doctor said I could talk to you for a few minutes."

Struggling with each breath, he continued to stare at her, his face a blank. At his side the machinery that kept his life going whirred and beeped and ticked, punctuating each rasping intake of air. The table covered with photographs and floral arrangements still stood at the foot of the bed.

"It's okay, Grandpa," Helen said. "You don't have to say anything." Helen reached over and picked up the photograph of the police officers at the barbecue. "I've been doing some thinking."

"What about?" he wheezed.

Still studying the picture, she turned so that he could see her face. "Lots of things, Grandpa. This picture, for one. This man standing on the left — that's Hal Watson, isn't it?"

"Heard about old Hal. Jimmy Davidson stopped by. Told me yesterday." He looked up at the ceiling. "Everyone but me gone now." A sound came out, a caricature of a laugh, that caused his chest to heave.

Helen sat down again, resting the picture on her lap. "Interesting — how all of you have these little hatbands. Each one a different color. That wasn't part of the uniform, was it, Grandpa?"

Except for the uneven breathing he lay perfectly still, his eyes fixed on the white cork tiles of the ceiling.

Helen went on. "It was the safe deposit box you meant. The last time Beth and I came here, right before they evacuated the town. I thought you were telling me to 'keep' Aunt Ruth's things, but you were really trying to say 'key.' "

"Knew it, all along. Knew something hidden in it," he said in a rough whisper. "What — letter? Papers?" He moved his head so he could look at her again.

In reply Helen opened her shoulder bag and showed him what she'd found in the safe deposit box. "This piece of cloth was stuck in the hinge of the box," she said, holding it out with both hands so he could see. "I didn't realize what it meant at first. All of you in the picture had one, sitting right there on your hats. It was like some kind of merit badge, or proof that you'd done it." Helen spoke the words quietly, as if they were discussing the menu for lunch, all the time watching her grandfather carefully for any signs of disturbance.

"And then there was Hal Watson," she continued. "It was what Don said to him, right before Hal killed him. It sounded as though Don believed he was carrying on something his uncle had started. But he was talking about the murders of those girls. It all made sense when I realized what this piece of cloth was."

He listened peacefully, more curious than upset. "You don't remember. Back then. Too little. Worst thing is, I didn't kill Mattie." He managed a wry grin. "You don't believe me, but it's true."

Stopping frequently to catch his breath, he got the story out in fragments. As soon as he'd left Joe Nathan that night, he'd gone in search of Mattie.

"The weather was a lot like it is now," he

recalled. "Hot and muggy, lotta rain. She was down by the Big Black, hidin'. Wasn't hard to find her, all the mess she made draggin' herself away."

Helen tensed as he coughed, his whole body racked with the pain. It was several minutes before he could speak again.

"Called out to her — didn't want to scare her — guess she was too shook up to do anything but keep runnin', poor child."

"Then what?" Helen asked after a long pause.

"Not sure. She must've slipped into the water, gotten tangled up in the weeds. Bunch of old logs stickin' out there, too. Could've hit her head on one of 'em. Too late by the time I found her. Rainin' pretty hard then, too."

Helen sighed and closed her eyes, trying to shut out the image of Mattie entangled in the water, fighting for her life. "So you buried her at Aunt Ruth's. Why? Why not just tell the truth?"

He shook his head against the pillows. "Already said — you don't know how it was. Everybody else had done theirs. All except me."

"Like membership in a club. Kill a nigger or you can't belong. Is that it?" The words, clanging with bitter disgust, were out before Helen could stop them. Shit, she swore to herself, hope this doesn't set him off.

But he seemed oblivious to her anger. He went on, talking to the ceiling, intent on getting it all out. "Election comin' up. Knew they'd make sure I'd lose if I didn't go ahead and do it. And I was scared of who they'd get into office. Figured I could keep things a little better by stayin' sheriff — try to control those boys, stop the beatin' and killin' wherever I could."

Helen fought to keep her voice even as he paused again. "How many, Grandpa? How many dead?"

He closed his eyes. "God knows," he breathed. "So many hurt, scared, dead, couldn't fight back. Didn't know what else to do."

"And what about Aunt Ruth? What did she think about all this?"

"Agreed with me. Knew there was no other way." He slowly raised himself on the bed so that he could look directly at Helen, pierce her with his glowing eyes. "That's all. Told 'em she was dead. Didn't say how. Ruth went along. Always."

Helen stood up, replaced the photograph, took a few paces around the room. She held her arms folded tight against her chest, hugging the information to herself. When she looked at her grandfather again, his face was drawn and gray but calm and relaxed. Resigned.

He took a deep breath. "What — what now?"

They stared at each other for several moments. Helen broke away first, turning to survey the array of medical equipment that stood between her grandfather and death. Soon enough, she knew, the pain would cease, the horrible gasping for air would stop, and all memory of what had happened would merge with infinity.

She looked back at his ravaged features, worn knife-thin from years of constant pain, each wrinkle chiseled into the wasted flesh. His trembling hands clutched uselessly at the sheets as he waited for her response.

Helen put the strip of cloth back into her purse

and snapped the fastener shut. "There are all kinds of punishment, Grandpa. Some are worse than others."

"Yes. Yes, child, you're right."

She turned on her heel and quickly left the room. As she walked down the hospital corridor, the doctors and nurses blurred against the white walls. Helen wiped the tears from her eyes and walked outside into the sweltering heat of the Mississippi summer.

Chapter Twenty-Two

"You talked to Frieda already?" Beth asked as she handed Helen the coffee.

"I called her this morning. She'll pick me up in San Francisco." They leaned against the railing and watched a plane take off, lifting and turning in the sun as it sped north in the shimmering heat. "It's going to be a long flight."

"How long do you think your grandpa has?"

Helen shrugged and stared into the plastic cup. "Maybe a few days, maybe longer. No one knows."

"Will you come back out then? When he's gone?"

Helen looked over at Beth, who was watching the runway. Was she imagining the note of pleading in Beth's voice? For the last few days, all the while Helen had finalized her arrangements about the house and prepared to go back home, Beth had been silent, concealing her feelings behind a cool exterior. Not for the first time, Helen wondered if she'd made a mistake the other day by the fireplace.

"I don't think so." On impulse she leaned against Beth, feeling her warmth, her solidity. "Why don't you come out to San Francisco, Beth?"

"Oh, one of these days I'll do the tourist thing, make it out to the land of fruits and nuts." Beth tried to laugh.

"No, I mean to stay. Get out of Mississippi for good."

Beth pulled away from her slightly. "I can't do that, Helen."

"Why not? What keeps you here?"

Beth smiled at her sadly. "I belong here, Helen. This place is me, with all its faults — and God knows it's got plenty. And don't start telling me how you did it, how you picked up and left and started over. You and I are different, Helen. I always knew you never belonged here. You were meant for other things, other places."

Helen listened, her stomach sinking as she recognized the truth in the words. "Are you angry at me about what happened the other day?" she asked quietly.

"Angry? For that beautiful afternoon?" Helen turned to see Beth's sad smile again. "How could I be angry with you for healing the past? That's what went on between us, Helen — somehow we got rid of the hurt we'd both been saving up all those years."

Helen looked down again, afraid she'd lose the battle to control her emotions. As she swallowed down the bitter coffee, an announcement boomed across the terminal, warning of a last call for the flight to San Francisco.

"Funny," Beth said as they made a path through the crowd. "I can't imagine Pemberton Road without a McCormick on it."

"I think Ray Pilkington and his community service projects will make much better residents than the McCormicks ever were." Helen pulled her bag over her shoulder and adjusted the strap. Should she have told Beth what she'd uncovered about her grandfather? Once again she decided it was best to leave it a secret, let it die with him. "I guess Ray is going ahead with plans for an open house there next month?"

"I'll be there." Beth watched her display her ticket to the agent, then pulled her aside before Helen could walk onto the ramp that led to the plane. The other passengers surged by as they exchanged one brief, fierce hug. "Good-bye, Helen." Beth pressed her lips swiftly to Helen's cheek.

Then she was gone, striding rapidly away from the boarding gate, away from the hordes of people scurrying toward the plane. Wordlessly, Helen watched her go.

Beth smiling at her, Beth's final kiss, Beth moving away from her — the images cycled through her mind as the plane lifted from the ground and headed west, into the sun, toward home.

A few of the publications of

THE NAIAD PRESS, INC.
P.O. Box 10543 • Tallahassee, Florida 32302
Phone (904) 539-5965
Toll-Free Order Number: 1-800-533-1973
Mail orders welcome. Please include 15% postage.

OPEN HOUSE by Pat Welch. 176 pp. P.I. Helen Black's fourth case.	ISBN 1-56280-102-3	$10.95
ONCE MORE WITH FEELING by Peggy J. Herring. 240 pp. Lighthearted, loving romantic adventure.	ISBN 1-56280-089-2	10.95
FOREVER by Evelyn Kennedy. 224 pp. Passionate romance — love overcoming all obstacles.	ISBN 1-56280-094-9	10.95
WHISPERS by Kris Bruyer. 176 pp. Romantic ghost story	ISBN 1-56280-082-5	10.95
NIGHT SONGS by Penny Mickelbury. 224 pp. A Gianna Maglione Mystery. Second in a series.	ISBN 1-56280-097-3	10.95
GETTING TO THE POINT by Teresa Stores. 256 pp. Classic southern Lesbian novel.	ISBN 1-56280-100-7	10.95
PAINTED MOON by Karin Kallmaker. 224 pp. Delicious Kallmaker romance.	ISBN 1-56280-075-2	9.95
THE MYSTERIOUS NAIAD edited by Katherine V. Forrest & Barbara Grier. 320 pp. Love stories by Naiad Press authors.	ISBN 1-56280-074-4	14.95
DAUGHTERS OF A CORAL DAWN by Katherine V. Forrest. 240 pp. Tenth Anniversay Edition.	ISBN 1-56280-104-X	10.95
BODY GUARD by Claire McNab. 208 pp. A Carol Ashton Mystery. 6th in a series.	ISBN 1-56280-073-6	9.95
CACTUS LOVE by Lee Lynch. 192 pp. Stories by the beloved storyteller.	ISBN 1-56280-071-X	9.95
SECOND GUESS by Rose Beecham. 216 pp. An Amanda Valentine Mystery. 2nd in a series.	ISBN 1-56280-069-8	9.95
THE SURE THING by Melissa Hartman. 208 pp. L.A. earthquake romance.	ISBN 1-56280-078-7	9.95
A RAGE OF MAIDENS by Lauren Wright Douglas. 240 pp. A Caitlin Reece Mystery. 6th in a series.	ISBN 1-56280-068-X	9.95
TRIPLE EXPOSURE by Jackie Calhoun. 224 pp. Romantic drama involving many characters.	ISBN 1-56280-067-1	9.95